Sporting Wood

Men in Love and Lust #3

Michael Bracken

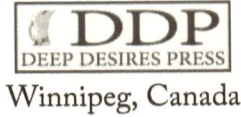

DDP
DEEP DESIRES PRESS

Winnipeg, Canada

Published October 2023 by Deep Desires Press, an imprint of Story Perfect Inc.

Deep Desires Press
PO Box 51053 Tyndall Park
Winnipeg, Manitoba R2X 3B0
Canada

Visit http://www.deepdesirespress.com for more scorching hot erotica and erotic romance.

For Temple
My Love, My Muse, My Everything

CONTENTS

INTRODUCTION

A good story is a good story, whether it has erotic content or not. And the pieces included in this collection are good stories.

Of course, I may be prejudiced, because several of them were included in anthologies I edited for Cleis Press. But the experience of putting together those volumes, as well as writing my own gay erotica, has given me a good sense of what makes a story sexy, intriguing, and worth reading.

My first published story, under the pseudonym Dirk Strong, was called "The Cop Who Caught Me" and sold to *Mandate*, a gay magazine that combined sexy picture layouts with erotic fiction. That was over thirty years ago, and writing that story, and many others, gave me the entrée I needed to begin editing those Cleis anthologies.

A good story needs to be well-written. Michael Bracken writes strong, propulsive sentences with great descriptions that bring the reader right into the characters' bedrooms—or wherever else they're getting it on.

The book is divided into two sections, Work and Play, and in both sections the description and the language take us right into the story. Here's a bit from the first story in the collection, "Landmark Photography," about discovering a great-grandfather's trove of erotic male photographs.

> One of the earliest prints to catch our attention had been taken near the end of WWII and featured a young sailor in his dress whites leaning against a public restroom sink, his white "Dixie Cup" hat pushed back at a jaunty angle, his highly polished black oxfords reflecting the camera's flash. The broadfall front of his bell-bottom uniform trousers had been half unbuttoned and his erect cock thrust upward through the opening.
>
> Kneeling before the sailor was an older man in a dark pinstripe suit, his fedora sitting on the sink atop a leather attaché case. A large handkerchief protected his knees from the tile floor, he had one hand on the sailor's hip away from the camera, and the other hand on the sailor's knee in front. He had his eyes closed, his mouth open, and was about to wrap his lips around the head of the young man's erect cock.

Not only do we get a sexy scene, but we're immediately transported to a different place and time, when "Even possession of my great grandfather's photographs carried a risk that must have proven quite a turn-on."

A later excerpt from the same story shows a different time and place.

> The hippie wore a loose-fitting, wildly patterned dashiki, a string of beads, and apparently nothing else. Vertically striped bellbottoms had been thrown over one corner of the statue's base, one belled leg hanging nearly to the ground above a pair of sandals, and the hippie braced himself with one hand against one of the statue's legs. He wore the police officer's flat-billed cap and had turned his head to look over his shoulder so we could see his face despite his pale, shoulder-length hair.
>
> The officer behind him had stripped off his uniform slacks and BVDs, leaving them on the ground nearby. He stood in black brogues with his dark socks held in place by garters fastened just below his knees, and he still wore his uniform shirt and his duty belt, complete with baton, handcuffs, magazine pouch, and holstered sidearm hanging from it. With a firm grip on the hippie's waist, his fat cock was already plunged halfway into the younger man's ass.

You can't get language more evocative of time and

place than that. Here's another example, from the story "Young Man's Game."

> Soon I sat on the tailgate with my jeans and my briefs bunched around my boots, and Carson stood before me. I leaned back on the pickup's bed, bracing myself with my hands, my erect cock jutting up like a saddle horn from the graying thatch of my pubic hair.
>
> When the photographer bent forward and took the swollen head of my cock in his mouth, I saw the last vestiges of the sun slip behind the horizon, and I moaned with pleasure. He licked away the glistening drop of pre-come, painted the head of my cock with his tongue, and then slowly took my entire length into his oral cavity.

The situations are inventive, from Steve and Marc copying the locations in Steve's great-grandfather's photos to the window-washer in "High-Rise Hookup" who spies on two men having sex while he's strung on his bosun's chair—and then later using that chair in a sexual encounter with the apartment owner. Then there's the sexually frustrated Texas mailman in "Total Package" who knows everything about those on his route from what he delivers—including a lot of paper-wrapped magazines to one customer in particular. Then there's Bob, the fifty-something rehab patient in "Heart On" who has this exchange with his therapist.

When he leaned forward and whispered in my ear, my physical therapist provided a workout incentive that I had not anticipated when I'd shuffled into the rehab center an hour earlier. "I'd fuck you so hard your heart would break the EKG."

"Is that a promise?"

"Get well," Trevor said as he straightened, "and we'll see what happens."

Readers will certainly be cheering for Bob's recovery!

The variety of language is one of the delights of the collection and says so much about the characters. The descriptions of sex are great, too, as in this example from "One-Hit Wonder." "While he kissed me, I untied the leather thong that held his pants closed, and then I forced my hand inside, finding his thick, erect cock and heavy ball sac."

Another of the delights of this collection is the way it moves so seamlessly from the historical to the contemporary, all the while taking us on an erotic journey rooted in characters so real they jump off the page.

That's important to the reader. We want to feel immersed in stories about real people who have great sex—something we might strive for ourselves, if only we meet the right guy who has the right equipment.

It's no surprise that Bracken has written and published so many stories in so many venues, and has frequently won awards and been short-listed for others.

Aging models, working men, college professors—whatever your interest, you'll find it within these pages. And I hope you'll enjoy them.

—Neil S. Plakcy
Hollywood, Florida

WORK

LANDMARK PHOTOGRAPHY

My great grandfather spent much of his life as an amateur photographer and had converted his detached two-car garage into a combination darkroom and studio long before my great grandmother left him following the birth of their only child. He never accepted digital photography, remaining addicted to film until his death in his mid-90s. Though he sent his color work to a professional lab, he developed his own black-and-white photos in the garage and even made his own prints. What none of us knew until my boyfriend and I began cataloguing his extensive collection of photographs and negatives was that my great grandfather wasn't just the family's go-to guy for birthdays, graduations, and weddings—he had also created a massive cache of explicit black-and-white man-on-man images.

While the rest of the family worked through great grandfather's house, Marc and I had been tasked with cleaning out his studio because I was the "artistic one," having had a few poems published in literary journals. Marc and I had come out to our working-class families long before we met and began cohabitating as graduate students, but my great grandfather's sexual orientation had been one of my family's best-kept secrets—and until we'd found his collection of photographs, I'd never suspected his personal peccadilloes.

After a brief discussion, Marc and I decided not to tell my family about the explicit black-and-white prints and negatives we'd discovered, of which there seemed to be thousands. Some of them had been taken in the garage studio or other private space, but many more caught pairs of men *in flagrante delicto* in public places where the participants risked capture by someone or something other than my great grandfather's camera. During the eras when the men were photographed, they risked social ostracism, incarceration, and physical assault for their sexual activities. Even possession of my great grandfather's photographs carried a risk back then—a risk that must have proven quite a turn-on.

One of the earliest prints to catch our attention had been taken near the end of WWII and featured a young sailor in his dress whites leaning against a public restroom sink, his white "Dixie Cup" hat pushed back at a jaunty angle, his highly polished black oxfords reflecting the camera's flash. The broadfall front of his bell-bottom uniform trousers had been half unbuttoned and his erect cock thrust upward through the opening.

Kneeling before the sailor was an older man in a dark pinstripe suit, his fedora sitting on the sink atop a leather attaché case. A large handkerchief protected his knees from the tile floor, he had one hand on the sailor's hip away from the camera, and the other hand on the sailor's knee in front. He had his eyes closed, his mouth open, and was about to wrap his lips around the head of the young man's erect cock.

Marc was sitting on a low stool when he found the photo and called me over to examine it with him. As I stood behind my lover and rested my hands on his shoulders, I was so close that my rapidly inflating erection stretched my jeans and pressed against his spine. He tossed the folder containing the print of the sailor and the businessman onto the counter before him, then spun around and reached for my zipper.

I pushed his hand aside. "My family's in the house…"

"They won't come out here," Marc said as he drew my zipper down. "They're tearing the house apart looking for the treasure they think your great grandfather hid. Out here it's just you and me and his 'stupid hobby.'"

He reached in and unthreaded my thick cock from the Y-front of my briefs. After he freed my erection, Marc bent forward, took my cock head in his mouth, and caught his teeth behind the swollen glans. He painted the head with his tongue while massaging my heavy ball sac. As he slowly took my entire length into his mouth, I stared at the photograph of the businessman and the sailor, wondering what had prompted them to meet in a public restroom and why my great grandfather had been present to photograph their encounter. I imagined myself as that sailor, smirking and gazing directly into the camera lens, perhaps on leave before being shipped overseas, while Marc was the businessman giving his young lover a memorable farewell in the bus station.

I drew back until my swollen glans caught behind Marc's teeth and then I pushed forward until my entire length once again filled his oral cavity. I did it again and again.

Outside the garage studio, one of my aunts called my name. "Steven!"

I stiffened, my rhythm interrupted for a fraction of a second, but I couldn't stop. I grabbed the back of Marc's head, catching my fingers in his blond hair, and quickly finished, erupting in his mouth and sending a thick stream of hot come against the back of his throat as I heard the side door open.

"I'll be out in a minute!" I called back.

My boyfriend swallowed, wiped come from the corner of his mouth with the back of his hand, and then spun around. He closed the folder of photographic prints we'd just been examining while I shoved my still-spasming cock into my pants and zipped up before pushing through the revolving darkroom door to find my aunt standing in the studio amidst my great grandfather's camera equipment.

"You two want lunch?" she asked. "We're sending your cousin to Mickey D's."

After that, we concentrated on sorting through the innocuous color prints and negatives whenever my relatives were nearby, often exchanging smiles over the thrill of what we had just done. We worked our way through innumerable family portraits, sunsets, and random photographs of public places until we realized that many of the seemingly random photographs had been taken as a form of pre-planning for the more adventurous black-and-white images. I recognized two pictures of the restroom where the sailor and the businessman had been photographed and Marc found a local landmark—the statue of a revolutionary war hero that graced our town square—where my great grandfather had photographed at least one couple every decade.

As we organized them, we showed the color photographs to my family. Although a few relatives wanted prints in which they or their immediate families were featured, none were interested in the bulk of the collection, so when my great grandfather's will was probated a few months later, I—with a feigned show of reluctance—took all the prints and negatives in lieu of cash disbursement from the assets of the estate salet.

Marc and I rented a truck and moved my great grandfather's photography files from his garage studio into the spare bedroom of a little bungalow we'd purchased the previous year. Until then the room had contained only a worktable and a stool where I'd sat to write my mostly unpublished poetry. It was there we spent much of our spare time working through all the prints and negatives, a task became easier when we found several handwritten notebooks that provided clues to the dates, locations, and identities of some of the participants.

Several weeks after moving everything into our place, we found another print that revved our engines. Taken in the mid-1950s, it featured a greaser and what appeared to be a mechanic in the service bay of an auto shop. The mechanic, a square-faced, middle-aged man with a flat-top and a jagged scar on the side of his chin, leaned forward and braced himself with one hand on the front fender of a '32 Ford 3-window coupe that had been chopped, channeled, and painted with flames extending from the grill all the way down the side to the rear fender.

Though he wore a sweat-stained undershirt, the mechanic's coveralls and briefs were pooled around his ankles. His thick cock dangled from the nest of dark hair at his crotch, and he thrust his ass toward the man standing behind him, a twenty-something greaser with long, dark hair slicked back into a duck's ass. The greaser wore a black leather jacket over a white undershirt, jeans with the cuffs rolled up several inches, and black high-top Chuck Taylor All Stars. With one hand on the mechanic's ass and the other holding the base of his erection, he appeared about to plunge his cock into the mechanic's tailpipe, and we wondered what the two men had found in the garage to use as lube because the greaser's cock glistened with reflected light.

We imagined that a love of cars, of customizing and driving souped-up rods, had brought these two men together—something we would never understand as the owners of a factory-stock hybrid—and we wondered how they had known my great grandfather and why they had invited him to one of their assignations in the garage.

As Marc and I examined the photograph and discussed what the two men might have been thinking that night so long ago, we both became aroused. I took Marc's face between my hands, feeling the rough stubble of his five o'clock shadow against my palms, and kissed him long and deep and hard. Marc was still dressed for work in navy blue chinos and a blue-striped seersucker shirt while I wore the same jeans and black T-shirt I had pulled on that morning. I fumbled open the buttons of his shirt and pushed it off his shoulders before I peeled off my T-shirt.

Marc stepped out of his tassel loafers and our pants hit the floor next. His cock tented silk boxers while mine stood free because I had gone commando that morning, and soon his underwear joined our pants and shirts. He wrapped his fist around my cock and began stroking it, but I wanted more, so I spun him around and bent him over the worktable. Because I couldn't be bothered to cross the hall to retrieve the lube we kept on the nightstand, I grabbed some hand lotion from the worktable, squirted a huge dollop into my palm, and then slathered it up and down Marc's ass crack.

I teased his hole with the lotion-slickened tip of my middle finger, pushing it into his ass as he relaxed. Usually I worked slowly, massaging his sphincter until I could ease a second finger into him before replacing my fingers with my cock, but I was too horny and too impatient to wait that long. I withdrew my finger, stepped behind Marc, and pressed my cock head against his ass hole. Then I grabbed his hips and thrust forward, burying the full length of my erection deep inside him.

I pulled back until just the head of my cock remained inside and then I thrust forward again. As I drew back and thrust forward, Marc reached down and wrapped his fist around his own erection. While I fucked his ass, he pistoned his fist up and down the length of his cock, matching me stroke-for-stroke until he couldn't wait and began fist-fucking himself faster than I was working his ass.

The streetlight in the alley behind our bungalow came on, surprising us, but not stopping us. We had been so aroused by the photograph of the greaser and the mechanic that we had failed to notice that the shades were up and that anyone traveling the alley behind our house could look in and see what we were doing. But we weren't about to stop—I had a firm grip on Marc's hips and my cock deep in his ass, and I was driving in and out of him like a hot rod piston.

He came first, luckily firing his thin stream of come into the cup of his hand and not on my great grandfather's black-and-white prints. And then, with one last, powerful thrust, I came, sending hot come deep inside my lover's shit chute.

I stood rigid behind him for a moment and then slowly relaxed until I was draped over Marc's back, my spasming cock slowly shrinking until it finally withdrew itself from the tight grip of his sphincter.

Only then did I draw the shades.

After several months of effort, we had just about finished examining all the prints when we found one more that we thought was far out. Taken during the late 1960s at the foot of the revolutionary war hero statue in our town square, it featured a beefy police officer and a slender, longhaired hippie flashing a two-fingered peace sign at the camera.

The hippie wore a loose-fitting, wildly patterned dashiki, a string of beads, and apparently nothing else. Vertically striped bellbottoms had been thrown over one corner of the statue's base, one belled leg hanging nearly to the ground above a pair of sandals, and the hippie braced himself with one hand against one of the statue's legs. He wore the police officer's flat-billed cap and had turned his head to look over his shoulder so we could see his face despite his pale, shoulder-length hair.

The officer behind him had stripped off his uniform slacks and BVDs, leaving them on the ground nearby. He stood in black brogues with his dark socks held in place by garters fastened just below his knees, and he still wore his uniform shirt and his duty belt, complete with baton, handcuffs, magazine pouch, and holstered sidearm hanging from it. With a firm grip on the hippie's waist, his fat cock was already plunged halfway into the younger man's ass, making it one of the few prints that showed penetration of any kind.

Staring at the photograph of the cop fucking the hippie's ass gave me a rock-hard erection that strained the crotch of my jeans. When Marc noticed, he reached for my zipper.

I shoved his hand away. "Not here."

"Then where?"

I stabbed my finger at the photograph in front of us. "There."

Marc stared at me for a moment and then a smile slowly spread across his face.

Since Marc and I had never had sex in a public place, we weren't entirely certain how to prepare. We changed into running shoes, T-shirts, and loose-fitting sweatpants that would be easy to slip off and slip back on. We looked like joggers. We were so excited about what we were about to do that our pants remained tented during the drive downtown.

Midnight was only minutes away when we arrived, and we parked near the plaque that identified the town square as some sort of historic location. The town's shopping district had long ago moved to the mall by the highway, and many of the buildings surrounding the square were empty. The remaining businesses had been closed for hours. Still, downtown was not completely abandoned. A few blocks in every direction were homes and apartment buildings, and traffic did occasionally pass by.

We left everything in the hybrid except my car keys, iPhone, and a tube of lube, and headed toward the statue. An overcast sky blocked most of the reflected light from the waning moon, and trees still grasping their fall foliage prevented the streetlights at the corners of the square from illuminating the center. Once we reached the statue, we looked around until we were satisfied that we were alone.

We started slow, kissing with closed mouths. Then we stopped, looked around, and kissed again. Before long

Marc's lips parted and I slipped my tongue between his teeth. Our kisses grew harder and deeper.

The more turned on we got, the less attention we paid to our surroundings, and soon Marc dropped to his knees in front of me, hooking his thumbs in the waistband of my sweatpants and pulling them to my ankles as he lowered himself. He cupped my heavy ball sac in one hand and wrapped his other fist around the base of my massive hard-on. Then he took the head of my cock in his mouth and spanked it with his tongue.

As he kneaded my nut sac, he slowly took the first few inches of my cock into his mouth, stopping when his lips reached his fist, and then drawing back. He did that several times, and soon I was trying to push his fist aside so that I could sink the entire length of my cock into his mouth, but he wouldn't let me.

When I thought I couldn't stand any more of his teasing, Marc released his oral grip on my cock and stood. He dropped his sweatpants to his ankles, handed me the lube, and turned to face the statue.

As he bent forward and grabbed the statue's leg the way the hippie had in the photo we'd been aroused by less than an hour earlier, I squirted a glob of lube on my fingers, covered my erection with it and then worked more of it into Marc's ass crack. I inserted first one finger and then two.

"Quit teasing me," he ordered huskily as he looked back over his shoulder.

I quickly replaced my fingers with my cock. The mushroom cap of my lube-slickened erection slipped into him with minimal resistance, and then I drove my entire shaft into his ass. I drew back and plunged forward again and again.

As we fucked in front of the statute, I held my iPhone at arm's length and took pictures of us until my impending orgasm changed the focus of my attention. I already had hold of one of Marc's hips, and I grabbed the other, capturing my iPhone between his skin and my palm. I slammed my cock into him again and again and again, faster and harder, and when I could no longer hold back, I came. I came hard into his ass.

We didn't have much time to enjoy a post-coital moment because we saw headlights flicker through the surrounding trees as a car approached the square from Main Street and then turned onto First Avenue to circumnavigate the square. As we quickly pulled up our sweatpants and hurried to the car, I did my best to ignore the come still oozing from my half-deflating cock.

We had just opened the hybrid's doors when a patrol car slid to a halt behind it and the police officer inside rolled down his window.

"Evening," he said with a nod.

"Evening, Officer," Marc responded.

"You two doing all right tonight?"

"Yes, sir," I replied. I kept my open car door between us so he couldn't see the throbbing bulge in my sweatpants or the rapidly spreading wet spot at my crotch.

"Nice evening for a jog," he said. "But you two might want to be careful. Downtown isn't a safe place at night.

You never know what kind of people you'll run into in the square."

After we assured him that we had been careful and that we were about to leave, he drove away.

We tumbled into bed as soon as we were home, laughing as we flipped through the photos I'd taken. They were poorly framed, poorly lit, out-of-focus, and the only record we had of what we'd just done.

"Your great grandfather would be so proud," Marc teased.

"Of my photography?"

"Of your sense of adventure," he said. "I never knew you had it in you."

We framed our three favorite prints from my great grandfather's collection and hung them in our bedroom where they would provide us with repeated visual stimulation. We didn't think much more about them until we hosted a holiday party for several of our friends, most of whom requested a tour of the place.

One of Marc's friends, a gallery owner named Felix, seemed blasé about the tour until we reached the bedroom and he spied my great grandfather's photographs on the wall. He stopped to stare at the image of the greaser and the mechanic before carefully examining all three prints. After he finished, he turned to me and asked, "Where did you get these?"

I told the story. He asked if I had more, so I walked him across the hall to the other bedroom, opened the door, and revealed a room packed wall-to-wall and floor-to-ceiling with filing cabinets and storage boxes filled with my great grandfather's life's work.

"May I look through these?"

"Help yourself," I told him. "I have to get back to the party."

We didn't see Felix again until most of the other guests had bid *adieu,* and we might not have seen him then if I hadn't gone looking.

He sat on a stool poring over a dozen prints he had arranged on the worktable. When he spun around, I saw his erect cock bulging in his chinos.

He peppered me with questions, asking if any of the photographs had ever been posted on the Internet, had ever been published, or had ever been displayed in a museum, gallery, or other public setting. I told him that as best I knew they never had been. Then he wanted assurance that I owned not only the physical prints and negatives but the copyrights as well.

I was able to assure him that I did. "Why?"

"Your great grandfather is the undiscovered Ansel Adams of gay porn," he said. "He chronicled decades of gay encounters, and his photography is impeccable."

Felix insisted that we display my great grandfather's work in his gallery, and, with his guidance during the coming weeks, we found a company to produce high-quality, large-format prints. The gallery opening that spring proved so successful I gave up writing poetry and concentrated on managing my great grandfather's posthumous photography career.

That initial gallery showing in Felix's gallery led to bigger exhibitions showings in other cities across the country and then to a coffee table book released as *Landmark Photography: A Pictorial History of Gay Sex in the 20th Century,* featuring text I had written.

Not only did my great grandfather's photographs provide Marc and me with a steadily growing income, but they also inspired us to continue experiencing sex outside the comfort and safety of our own home.

We fucked in a service station while on a trip across state, we fucked in the confessional before his sister's wedding, we fucked in the dugout of our town's minor league baseball team, as well as in dozens of other public locations where we tempted discovery. The possibility that we might get caught acted like a psychological Viagra, making my cock stiffer than ever, and our sex was always hard, fast, sweaty, and captured in pixels.

We started using a high-quality digital camera mounted on a tripod to capture our public misadventures. Our photographs weren't ever as good as my great grandfather's, but we quickly gained an appreciation for the art of stealth during semi-public sex and looking through the photos later always turned us on.

In our own way, we carried on my great grandfather's secret hobby by posing for our own indecent exposures.

HIGH-RISE HOOK-UP

Joe Nelson sat in a bosun's chair thirty-two stories above the street, cleaning the windows of a high-rise condominium. Using a figure-eight motion, he slid a soapy brush over the glass pane before him. Then he repeated the motion with a squeegee, flicked soapy water from the squeegee, and moved to the next window. Two sixty-pound ropes attached to permanent tiebacks on the roof prevented him from plummeting to his death. The main rope was attached to the bosun's chair upon which he sat, and the other rope was affixed to the safety harness strapped around his torso. In addition to the brush and the squeegee, hanging from the bosun's chair or from his utility belt were a ten-gallon bucket filled with soapy water, a spray bottle of cleaning solution, and a scraper to clear away bird shit and other sticky substances.

As he moved from window to window, Joe used a single suction cup grabber to stabilize himself. Sometimes the sound of the suction cup thudding against the window startled people on the other side of the glass, but for the most part the condominium's residents ignored the window washer's presence outside their window, just as the people working inside office buildings did. For that reason, he often saw things he should not have seen, from people fast asleep at their desks in the middle of the workday to others in various stages of undress moving about in the false privacy of their homes. Joe usually ignored what he saw because the Peeping Tom aspect of his job wasn't what had drawn him to window cleaning—he had been attracted by the significant increase in pay from his previous position as a janitor—but sometimes he couldn't help himself.

Joe had just finished cleaning someone's living room window and had swung into position to clean the next window when he found himself staring into a bedroom where two naked men were enjoying the pleasure of one another's company. Neither seemed aware of his presence and neither reacted to the thud of his suction cup against the glass. Perhaps because they were in the bedroom of a condominium unit that cost more than he would earn in his lifetime, Joe suspected they were gentlemen he would never encounter in the blue-collar bars where he spent his off hours cruising for companionship.

The slender, dark-haired younger of the two men knelt on the plush carpet with his back to the window and with the older man's cock in his mouth. The older man's black hair had gone gray at the temples, and he had the thickset build of someone who spent much of his time sitting behind a desk. Though the older man faced Joe, his eyes were closed, and he had his thick fingers wrapped around the back of the younger man's head. He thrust his hips forward and back, pistoning his cock in and out of the other man's mouth.

Joe knew he should wash the window and move on, but he hesitated. As he watched the two men, his cock grew rigid, and he became increasingly uncomfortable because the safety harness was not compatible with tight blue jeans and a hard-on. The tempo of the older man's hips increased, and Joe could tell from the look on his face that he was about to come. The window washer wanted to pull his cock out of his pants and come with the older man but there was no way that would happen while he was hanging thirty-two stories above the street. Instead, he just watched until the older man slammed his hips against the younger man's face one last time and his entire body tensed with orgasm.

A moment later the older man opened his eyes, pulled his softening cock from the other man's mouth, and saw Joe hanging outside the window. Joe immediately splashed soapy water on the glass and made an incomplete figure eight with his brush. As he squeegeed off the soapy water, the younger man moved to cover himself and the older man crossed the room to stand naked only inches from the window. His thick, saliva-slickened cock hung between his thighs, a thin string of come briefly swinging from the tip.

He stared into Joe's eyes for a moment. Then he said something over his shoulder that caused the younger man to reach into the inner breast pocket of one of the suit jackets before joining him at the window. A gold business card case exchanged hands. Then the older man opened it, removed a card, and pressed the face of it flat against the glass with the palm of his hand.

Joe stared at the card until he memorized the man's name, the name of his law firm, and his cellphone number. Then he dropped down to the next set of windows.

When the window washer dropped out of sight, Marcus Wainwright peeled his business card from the glass and turned away from the window. He'd been surprised to see someone watching him face-fuck the young paralegal from his law firm, but the surprise had quickly turned to interest when he realized the man watching them had a bulge in his jeans that warranted closer inspection. When he'd stood naked before the window staring into the pale blue eyes of the window washer, he'd recognized that the other man's desire wasn't limited to a little blood rushing to his crotch. The man hanging outside of his bedroom window made Wainwright think of a hunky piñata that needed to be whacked off until it erupted with come.

He'd made the paralegal fetch his business card case because he wanted the man outside to know the interest was mutual. He didn't know if the window washer would call, but he would certainly be the subject of Wainwright's erotic fantasies for some time to come. Thinking about being watched and imagining having his way with the muscular window washer gave him another erection, and he wanted to finish what had been interrupted. He said as much to the younger man as he replaced his business card in the gold case and tossed the case on the bed.

The paralegal pulled the curtains closed and then crossed the darkened room to the nightstand. From it he took a partially used tube of lube, squeezed a dollop into the palm of his hand, and wrapped his hand around Wainwright's stiff cock. He stroked his fist up and down the thick shaft until he had completely covered it with lube. He squeezed another dollop onto his fingertips, lifted his ball sac with his other hand, and coated his ass crack and anal opening with lube.

The paralegal turned and bent over the bed, supporting himself with his hands. Wainwright stepped up behind him and nestled his cock in the younger man's lube-slickened ass crack. He slid his cock up and down several times before he drew back and repositioned himself. He pressed the spongy soft head of his cock against the paralegal's ass hole and slowly pressed forward until the younger man opened to him.

After he eased his entire length into the paralegal, he drew back until just the head of his cock remained. Then he thrust forward and drew back with a steadily increasing rhythm. Wainwright grabbed the younger man's hips and fucked him hard and fast.

As the younger man accepted each of Wainwright's powerful thrusts, his own cock lengthened, stiffened, and strained with desire. He did nothing about it, and Wainwright continued pumping into his ass until he could no longer restrain himself. He slammed his hips against the younger man's buttocks one last time and then came. He fired a thick wad of warm spunk deep into the paralegal's ass, and they stood locked together until Wainwright's cock quit spasming and began to soften.

He stepped backward, withdrawing from the other man. When the paralegal straightened and turned, Wainwright ignored the younger man's erection and said, "We'd better hurry, or we'll be late to the deposition."

Joe worked his way to the ground one window at a time. As soon as his feet hit the sidewalk, he took his cell phone from his pocket and entered the name and phone number he had memorized earlier. Then he returned to the roof with a fresh bucket of soapy water, moved the safety ropes, and again worked his way down the side of the building.

He finished his assigned section of windows shortly before the rest of the crew finished theirs and was waiting when they humped their safety harnesses and cleaning equipment to the company van. During the ride back to the office, they shared what they had seen through the windows that day. Billy had seen six marijuana plants arranged under a grow light, John had watched a Chihuahua take a dump on someone's Persian Rug, and Carlos had watched a topless blonde vacuum her living room. The other guys peppered Carlos with questions about the blonde and never got around to asking Joe anything.

Watching one man perform a blow job on another had been the highlight of Joe's day. Just thinking about what he had seen made Joe's cock stir inside his jeans. He was so horny after clocking out, he drove straight to

Woody's, a hole-in-the-wall that had been catering to blue-collar men of his predilections since long before students from the nearby university discovered the place. Once inside, Joe straddled a stool at the bar, ordered a beer, and turned to scan the room while he drank. A dozen men like Joe, hired hands and blue-collar workers winding down at the end of the workday, had taken control of the darkened booths that lined two walls, and many of them already had a young companion. Students—alone and in twos and threes—sat at the tables arranged in the center of the room between the booths.

Joe had emptied his beer bottle when he caught the eye of a young man sitting alone at one of the tables nursing his own beer. He was drinking the same brand as the window washer, so Joe had the bartender open two bottles and he carried them to the table where the young man sat. He straddled an empty chair and slid one of the bottles across the table.

"Thanks," the young man said as he took a sip. "I haven't seen you before."

"I've been around," Joe said.

The young man asked what Joe did for a living and Joe told him he washed windows. The young man didn't seem impressed, so Joe added, "On the outside of skyscrapers."

The additional information piqued the young man's interest. "You must not be afraid of heights."

"As long as I'm careful, there's no reason to be afraid." Joe watched the young man's eyes to see if he caught the underlying message. When he felt certain that the young man had, he asked, "And you?"

"Law school. Second year."

"What a coincidence," Joe said. "I saw a couple of lawyers today who were getting into each others' briefs."

"Saw?"

Joe told him exactly what he'd watched while hanging outside the bedroom window. He knew his story aroused his young companion because the law student reached into his lap and adjusted the crotch of his pants.

"You must see a lot of things like that."

"Not as much as you'd think."

They talked for a few more minutes, during which they exchanged first names, before Joe excused himself to use the men's room. Just as he expected, Charles followed.

The window washer locked the door and unbuckled his belt. Then Charles pushed his hands aside, unbuttoned Joe's jeans, and slid down the zipper. He hooked his thumbs in the waistband of Joe's boxer briefs and tugged his briefs and his jeans down as he dropped to his knees.

Joe's cock had remained semi-erect ever since he completed his story about watching the two men in the condominium bedroom, and it pointed at Charles's face. Charles wrapped one hand around the thick shaft and pulled Joe's foreskin away from his cock head. Then he took half of Joe's cock into his mouth and drew back until the swollen glans caught against the back of his teeth.

Charles removed his fist from Joe's cock and pressed his face forward until he had the entire length of the window washer's cock in his mouth. He reached around and grabbed Joe's ass cheeks, his fingernails digging into Joe's skin as he bobbed his head forward and back.

Someone rattled the bathroom door, but they ignored it. Whoever it was would have to wait his turn. Joe began pumping his hips in counter-rhythm to the motion of the law student's head, but he wasn't completely in the moment. With his eyes closed, he replayed the condominium bedroom scene against the back of his eyelids. Whether Charles realized it or not, Joe was using the young man as a substitute for the men he'd seen in that bedroom.

When Joe felt his balls tighten and his cock stiffen, he knew he would not last much longer. He caught the back of Charles's head in his hands and held it as he thrust his cock deep into Charles's mouth several more times. When he came, he came hard. He fired a thick wad of warm come against the back of Charles's throat.

Charles swallowed repeatedly and then licked Joe's cock head clean before releasing his oral grip. While Charles pushed himself to his feet, Joe pulled up his pants and tucked himself away. With his stress relieved, Joe figured it was time to head home. When he told the law student that he needed to leave, Charles suggested they swap cell phone numbers.

The paralegal was a trifle with which Wainwright killed time, not someone with whom he felt any real connection. Young lawyers, paralegals, and law clerks were easy enough conquests because they often threw themselves at him in failed attempts to curry his favor. He used each of the sycophants in turn and moved on, fucking his way through the city's legal system like a Viagra-fueled satyr. And he felt unfulfilled.

What he wanted more than anything was a real man, one who did not cower before him or expect *quid pro quo* for their sexual favors. Who better than a man who dangled dozens of stories above the street with nothing but a bit rope to prevent him from certain death?

During the weeks following the window washer's appearance outside his bedroom window, Wainwright rebuffed the advances of three different men he had on his fuck-it list. His desire for sexual release only increased as he denied it of himself, and he wasn't usually one to self-pleasure with so much willing man-meat available. Even so, he found himself doing just that one Friday evening after rejecting yet another potential suitor. He lay naked on his bed with a tube of lube, a box of tissue, and memories of the man hanging outside his bedroom window. With the curtains wide open he could see the city at night and felt reasonably confident no one could see him in his darkened bedroom as he replayed in his mind the moment he'd first noticed the window washer staring through the window.

His cock began to lengthen and stiffen, so he squeezed a bit of lube into the palm of his hand, wrapped his fist around his erection, and stroked himself. As he continued stroking, Wainwright's gaze drifted around the room until it settled on the eyebolt the previous owner had installed in the bedroom ceiling. He imagined many possible uses for it, including a few that involved the window washer and his safety harness.

When his balls tightened and a bit of pre-come moistened the tip of his cock, Wainwright grabbed a wad of tissue. Just in time, he covered his cock head and caught the thick wad of spunk that shot out.

After a difficult day during which he had been attacked by an aggressive falcon nesting on the sill of a forty-third-floor window, Joe dialed Charles's phone number. The law student answered on the third ring, and they arranged to meet later that evening.

They didn't spend much time on preliminaries and were in Joe's bedroom less than ten minutes after Charles's arrival. The young man stripped first, leaving his clothes in a heap on the floor. He carried a bit of extra weight, had no tan, and had no visible hair below his neck.

Unlike his young companion, Joe had well-developed arms, shoulders, and chest from repeatedly maneuvering up, down, and across the face of skyscrapers throughout the city, and he made little effort to groom his limited body hair.

By the time the window washer had removed his clothing, both of their cocks stood erect. Charles stepped forward and took Joe's erection in his hand. He stroked his fist up and down the turgid shaft several times before he asked, "You have any lube?"

"On the headboard," Joe said, "next to the magazines."

Charles turned toward the bed, said nothing about the

stack of pornographic magazines he found there, and turned back toward Joe with the nearly empty tube of lube in his hand. Joe took it from the law student, applied some to his erection and then, when Charles turned to face away from Joe, to the young man's ass crack.

Joe massaged a glob of lube into Charles's sphincter, feeling his ass hole open as Charles relaxed. Joe eased one finger into him, and after a few moments eased in a second finger. Then he removed his fingers and pressed the head of his cock against Charles's anal opening. Joe grabbed his hips and thrust forward, driving his cock deep inside the young man. He drew back and did it again.

Joe pounded into Charles again and again and soon could not stop himself. With one last powerful thrust, he buried his cock inside the young law student and filled his ass with warm spunk. As he held the young man's ass tight against his crotch, he reached around and took Charles's cock in his fist. While he was still spasming within Charles, he fist-fucked the law student.

When Charles came and his cock spewed come over Joe's fist, his sphincter spasmed around Joe's semi-hard cock, almost as if milking the last drops of come from Joe. After Charles's sphincter stopped spasming, Joe slowly withdrew his cock and then collapsed on the bed. Charles joined him.

"Why do you do it?" Charles asked. "Why do you wash windows on skyscrapers?"

"After high school I worked for a janitorial service," Joe explained. "One day I was staring out the window when a guy rappelled down from the floor above and cleaned the window in front of me. Later, when I found out how much the job paid and that we were part of the same union, I started asking around."

"You don't do it for the thrill?"

"Thrill?" Joe asked. "It isn't mountain climbing, it's a job. The first time I dropped over the side of a building, I almost shit my pants."

Wainwright didn't answer his cellphone because he was in a meeting with a client and didn't recognize the number when he glanced at the caller ID. Later he listened to the message and heard an unfamiliar voice say, "I'll be washing the windows on your side of the condo tomorrow."

Several weeks had passed since his encounter with the window washer and his desire had only increased. He had his paralegal reschedule the next day's afternoon meetings.

Wainwright had just unlocked his front door when his cell phone announced an incoming text. Believing the message to be from a client or from his office, the attorney didn't check his phone until he reached his bedroom and peeled off his suit coat. When he did, the phone's screen filled with the image of Joe's thick cock and heavy ball sac dangling from a nest of sandy blond pubic hair. Wainwright's cock twitched with desire.

By the time Joe swung into view and his suction cup grabber thudded against the window, Wainwright had shed his clothes. He crossed the room to the window as he had the first time he'd spotted Joe outside his bedroom, and he stood before the glass with his semi-erect cock grasped firmly in his right hand.

He knew what caused the bulge in the window washer's tight-fitting jeans because he'd had time to appreciate the selfie before Joe's arrival. As Wainwright watched the window washer's eyes, the window washer watched him stroke himself. His cock didn't need much encouragement before it stood at attention. When it did, Wainwright released his grip and pressed his erection against the cool glass, rubbing it against the smooth surface as he pumped his hips up and down.

As Wainwright watched, Joe touched the other side of the glass near his ball sac, ran his finger up the length of Wainwright's cock, and then licked his lips. Wainwright stepped back, wrapped his fist around his cock again, and pumped hard and fast. When he came, he fired a thick wad of spunk that would have struck the window washer's face if glass had not separated them.

Joe watched the spunk slowly crawl down the window. He slid his soapy brush in a quick figure eight on the other side, repeated the motion with his squeegee, and flicked away the soapy water. Then he dropped down to the next set of windows and worked his way to the ground. He wasn't surprised to find the lawyer waiting for him when he reached the sidewalk.

"You put on quite a show, Mr. Wainwright," Joe said as he unfastened himself from the bosun's chair.

"Marcus," the attorney said. "Call me Marcus."

"So, what can I do for you, Marcus?"

"How about drinks at my place Saturday evening?"

"Nothing fancy," Joe said. He named his beer and they agreed on a time.

Wainwright started to walk away and then he turned back.

"Yes?" Joe asked.

"And bring your harness."

Joe arrived at Wainwright's condominium with his safety harness slung over his shoulder and was ushered into the living room where Wainwright had an ice bucket chilling three bottles of Joe's favorite beer. Wainwright had already opened on a bottle of wine for himself, and he poured himself a second glass while Joe put his gear on the floor and opened a beer.

Joe took his drink to the window and stared out at the city for a moment. Then he turned to his host. "Nice view," he said. "I never get to see it like this."

"You must see things other people never see." Wainwright said as he stepped up beside his guest.

"I usually see things I can't have," Joe said.

Wainwright rested his hand on Joe's arm, the first time the two men had any kind of physical contact. "I think that'll change soon."

They stared into each other's eyes for a moment, the first time they'd done that without a thick sheet of glass separating them. Wainwright reached up, ran the back of his hand along Joe's jawline, and then caught the back of

Joe's head in his palm. Then Wainwright pressed his lips against Joe's.

The kiss lasted only a moment but sent fire to their loins. They set aside their unfinished drinks and came together a second time, this kiss even deeper. Their tongues entwined, each fighting for dominance.

They both knew why Wainwright had invited Joe to his apartment. Wainwright had dealt with his desire by avoiding carnal contact with other men while Joe had dealt with his desire by fucking a young law student. The time had come to discover if their mutual desire survived the transition from fantasy to reality.

They peeled off one another's clothing, leaving it strewn around the living room and down the hall as they moved into the bedroom, each still attempting to establish dominance over the other until Joe had the attorney pressed flat against the bedroom window and stood with his erect cock nestled in Wainwright's ass crack.

"This why you showed me your card that day?" Joe whispered in the attorney's ear as he slowly pumped his hips forward and back.

"God, yes," Wainwright breathed huskily.

"Why the harness?"

The attorney pointed over his shoulder toward the ceiling and Joe glanced in that direction. He hadn't noticed the eyebolt when he'd watched Wainwright and the other man going at it several weeks earlier, nor when he'd watched Wainwright masturbate for him only a few days earlier, but he knew as soon as he saw it why Wainwright had insisted that he bring his safety harness.

"You sure it'll hold someone?"

"It'll hold at least 500 pounds," Wainwright said. "That's what the previous owner said. I've never tested it."

Joe had never had sex while hanging from his safety harness nor had he ever had sex with someone else hanging from a safety harness. He had never even considered it, but the idea intrigued him. He stepped back, removing his cock from the attorney's ass crack and allowing Wainwright to step away from the glass.

The window washer walked to the living room, returned with his safety harness, and strapped Wainwright into it. Then he stood on a chair to hook the harness to the eyebolt in the ceiling and lifted the attorney off his feet.

Joe moved the chair aside and turned back. Wainwright was slowly spinning in a circle, unable to stop himself. Joe grabbed the harness and reached between Wainwright's thighs. He grabbed the man's scrotum and kneaded the attorney's nuts as he stroked the sensitive spot behind the man's sac, almost, but not quite touching the attorney's anal opening.

"Stop teasing me," Wainwright said. "The lube's in the nightstand."

Joe crossed the room and returned with a new tube. He slathered his cock with the slick substance and then spun Wainwright around and pushed him forward until the attorney was horizontal, like a skydiver before pulling his chute open. Wainwright waved his arms, swimming in mid-air to keep from turning upside down.

Joe grabbed Wainwright's legs and spread them as he

stepped between the attorney's thighs. He coated Wainwright's ass crack with a thick glob of lube and then teased his anal opening with the tip of one finger.

Wainwright's ass slowly opened to Joe's digital probing. Joe slid his finger in and out of the other man several times before he eased in a second finger. When he felt certain the attorney was relaxed enough to take his entire length, Joe withdrew his fingers and pressed the swollen head of his cock against Wainwright's sphincter. He grabbed the attorney's hips and pulled him backward until the attorney was impaled on his stiff cock.

Using the pendulum motion of the safety harness, he pushed the attorney forward and pulled him back, quickly finding a rhythm that both men found enjoyable.

Wainwright was at the window washer's mercy and Joe knew it. He increased the speed of the swinging motion, pushing and pulling the attorney faster and faster until he felt his scrotum tighten and his cock stiffen, and he couldn't restrain himself. He pulled Wainwright's ass tight against him and fired a thick wad of warm spunk deep inside the attorney as Wainwright hooked his ankles together behind Joe's back.

He reached around the attorney and grabbed hold of his erection. He still had a little lube on his hand and he quickly fist fucked the hanging man, driving him toward a quick release that had the attorney firing his wad over the plush carpet.

As the attorney came, his sphincter spasmed around Joe's cock, milking the last of his come until Joe pushed the man away and stepped aside.

As Wainwright swung back and forth, he asked, "How do I get out of this thing?"

"You don't," Joe told him. "Not until I'm done with you."

Joe stepped out of the bedroom and returned with a fresh beer and Wainwright's unfinished glass of wine. He stopped the attorney, helped him straighten up, and handed him his drink.

They fucked, they drank, and they fucked more.

Half the night disappeared before they exhausted themselves and Joe released the attorney from the safety harness.

When Joe finally left Wainwright's place, his harness in hand, he knew he would never see his job the same way again.

And Wainwright planned to stop fucking his way through the legal system and spend more time with hard-working men who knew exactly how to work him.

ONE HIT WONDER

Ronnie tours the country under his stage name, playing with pick-up bands at every stop, a one-hit wonder who parlayed a guitar riff accidentally created at seventeen into five albums with four different recording companies and two decades of non-stop touring in the hope of someday recreating that one summer when he topped the charts, headlined large venues, and opened for stadium-filling supergroups.

He picked me up two years ago when the owner of a dive in Springfield wouldn't provide anyone to watch his merchandise table. I'd been standing in the back parking lot holding all five of Ronnie's CDs in my backpack when he arrived and stepped out of a dirty white minivan. Even in faded blue jeans and loose gray sweatshirt, with a pair of dark-framed glasses perched on the end of his nose and his shoulder-length black hair pulled into a loose ponytail, he still looked every bit the rock 'n' roll star he had been twenty years earlier. He graciously signed the CDs, asked if I was planning to attend the show later that night, and then disappeared through the back door.

I was walking away when I heard Ronnie's voice again.

"Hey, kid!"

I was no kid—I had just turned twenty-three—but I was the only person in the parking lot. I turned.

"You want to see the show for free and earn a few bucks?"

I could always use extra money. I lived in my parents' basement and worked part-time selling pretzels at the mall.

Ronnie told me what he needed and soon we were hauling boxes of CDs and T-shirts into the bar. The owner let us push two small tables together next to the stage, and I unpacked everything while Ronnie worked with the power trio that would be backing him that night, putting a little pop in their power.

That night the little stage couldn't contain Ronnie. Before the show he changed into black leather pants that bulged provocatively at the crotch, snakeskin cowboy boots, and a black T-shirt that he peeled off halfway through the night to reveal powerful biceps, broad chest, and washboard abs that I would not have expected on a thirty-seven-year-old man who spent his life driving from city to city in a minivan. I had come to the show because of his one hit, a power pop number about what it's like to be different—a song that had spoken to me in high school when I realized I wasn't like the other boys in my gym class. Watching him perform turned me on. The way he handled the guitar, stroking the long neck, his fingers flying over the strings, made my cock hard, and it pressed uncomfortably against the inside of my jeans.

I know I wasn't the only one turned on by Ronnie's performance. Some of the women—all of them Ronnie's age because people my age don't remember him or his two-week visit to the top of the pop charts—offered themselves to Ronnie during the breaks, not realizing, as I did, his groupie gender preference. They turned out to be his biggest fans, though, buying six T-shirts and almost three-dozen CDs.

"Not bad," Ronnie told me after the bar closed and we were packing to leave. He counted the money, separated out ten percent, and handed it to me.

I stuffed the cash in my pocket, carried his merchandise out to the minivan, grabbed my backpack, and started to walk away.

"Hey, kid," Ronnie said. "Where you headed?"

"Bus stop," I said. "Home."

He opened the minivan's passenger door. "Get in. I'll take you."

I knew from the way he looked at me that he had something else in mind. I also knew when I climbed in the passenger seat and closed the door that I was thinking the same thing.

Ronnie drove to a motel near the highway, a place that had seen better days but was still clean and well maintained, and invited me inside for a drink. He carried his Les Paul in with us but left everything else in the minivan.

We never had the drink. As soon as the door closed

behind us and Ronnie leaned his guitar case against the wall, he pulled me into his arms and covered my lips with his. I opened my mouth and his tongue slid between my teeth. I sucked on it and sucked hard. Our kiss was long and deep, and when it ended my heart was pounding and my legs were weak, and I had to brace myself against the door to keep from falling over.

"You know why we're here, don't you?" Ronnie asked as he stared deep into my eyes.

I nodded.

"And you're okay with that?"

"I've dreamed about it."

"I'm usually careful," he continued. "I don't invite just anybody back to my room after a show."

Maybe he was telling the truth. Maybe he was lying. I didn't care. I wanted him and nothing he could say would change that.

I reached out, took his hand, and pulled him to me. Hoarsely, I whispered, "Stop talking."

He kissed me again, harder this time. While he kissed me, I untied the leather thong that held his pants closed, and then I forced my hand inside, finding his thick, erect cock and heavy ball sac.

My own cock was erect, but I was more concerned with pleasing Ronnie than with having my needs met. I grabbed the waistband of his leather pants and pulled them down as I dropped to my knees. To avoid underwear lines, he'd worn nothing beneath the pants and his erect cock rose majestically between us.

Ronnie still wore his snakeskin boots and, with his

leather pants pooled around his ankles and his balls in my mouth, he could hardly move. I had him where I wanted him. I leaned forward and sucked his nuts into my mouth, bathing his hairy sac with my tongue as his thick cock bobbed in front of my face. His nuts tasted of sweat and leather and his curly hair caught between my teeth.

After thoroughly coating his nut sac with my saliva, I licked the underside of his cock stem from the base to the spongy soft mushroom cap. Then I wrapped my fist around the stiff shaft and took the head of his cock into my mouth. I hooked my teeth behind the glans and teased the pee slit with the tip of my tongue. As I did that, I slowly pumped my fist up and down the length of his cock.

Ronnie was too horny to wait. He grabbed the back of my head, thrust his hips forward, and buried his cock in my mouth. His soggy ball sac slapped my chin as he drew back and thrust forward again and again.

He came quickly, firing a thick glob of hot spunk against the back of my throat. I swallowed, and then swallowed again.

When Ronnie's cock quit spasming in my mouth, he pulled away, stripped off his clothes, and dropped onto the king-size bed. He fell asleep before I had a chance to remove my clothes, and I took care of myself in the bathroom before I climbed into bed beside him.

We hit the road the next morning, on our way to Ronnie's next one-night-stand fronting yet another pick-up band of dubious talent.

All I had in my backpack were the five autographed CDs, a paperback mystery, and a couple of protein bars.

At an outlet mall in the middle of nowhere, just after we stopped for breakfast at a Cracker Barrel, Ronnie bought me underwear, socks, and a pair of Levi's. When we returned to the minivan, he opened one of the merchandise boxes and gave me three of his T-shirts. Then he handed me his key ring and told me it was my turn to drive.

Just like that I became Ronnie's driver, roadie, merchandise manager, and lover.

I called my parents when we stopped for lunch, told them I had found a job as a traveling salesman, phoned my old boss and told her I wouldn't be returning to the pretzel stand, and then realized that no one else would care what had happened to me. The life I was leaving behind was no life at all.

During the following months I learned how to take care of Ronnie and he took care of me. The most important thing I learned is that Ronnie is always horny after a show, so we rocked and fucked our way across America, occasionally stopping at his sister's house in Tulsa to replenish the merchandise from the stash in her garage.

We usually stayed in cheap motels and ate fast food, but Ronnie's booking agent outdid himself a few weeks ago. He arranged a seven-night run at a casino where we stayed in a suite and had our meals comped. Ronnie performed every night on stage and in the bedroom.

When we returned to the suite after the final show on Sunday, Ronnie showered before joining me in the living area wearing nothing but a white hotel robe with a loosely tied sash. The hotel had sent up a chilled bottle of champagne and he uncorked it.

"It's our last night to live like rock stars," Ronnie said as he filled two champagne glasses. "Tomorrow we hit the road again."

After spending a week in a hotel suite, I wasn't looking forward to motoring from motel to motel in the minivan, and I said so.

"It'll probably never get any better than this," Ronnie said, "and it may be a long time before it gets this good again."

In two years together this was the first time I'd heard Ronnie admit that he might never again be the big star he had once been. I raised my champagne glass. "To tonight, then."

He lifted his glass in silent toast and then drained it. We drank until we emptied the bottle. When there was no more champagne, Ronnie threw his empty glass at the wall, where it shattered and rained pieces onto the carpet below.

He took my wrist and pulled me to him, slid his hands under my T-shirt, and teased my nipples with his thumbs. After I peeled my shirt off and threw it aside, Ronnie reached for my belt. Half a bottle of champagne wasn't enough to make him drunk, but it certainly caused his motor skills to deteriorate. I helped him with my belt. Then I kicked off my running shoes and peeled off the rest of my clothes.

"You're just as hot as the day I met you, kid," Ronnie said. He shook the robe from his shoulders and let it drop to the carpet at his feet. His cock was half-erect and growing.

The curtains were open but neither of us considered the possibility that anyone could see us so many floors up.

"Hot?" I asked. "I was just an innocent kid standing in the parking lot hoping to get an autograph." I stepped forward and grabbed his cock. "You gave me a lot more than that."

Ronnie had given me the ticket out of my torpid existence in Springfield, had shown me an America I never would have seen without him, and had taught me more about the bottom end of the music business than anyone should ever have to know. And all I had to do was be there when he wanted me.

He captured my head between his hands and planted a big kiss on my lips to shut me up. Immediately our tongues met in a fiery, alcohol-fueled dance of desire.

When the kiss finally ended, Ronnie reached down and dug through the pockets of the robe. When he stood, he held a tube of lube. He spun me around and bent me over the back of the couch, trapping my erect cock against the white leather.

Years of guitar playing had given him powerful fingers, and after he squeezed a thin trail of lube into the crack of my ass, he smeared the lube over the tight pucker of my ass. His fingers were so strong I couldn't have resisted even if I had wanted to, and he pushed one finger into me. A second finger followed the first and a moment later his cock head replaced his fingers.

After he eased the mushroom cap past my sphincter,

he grabbed my hips and drove his cock all the way into me. He pulled back and pushed forward, and as he did that my cock rubbed against the leather couch beneath me.

The friction of my cock against the leather was an unexpected treat, and I found myself enjoying the feeling of my cock against the couch as much as I enjoyed Ronnie rocking my world from behind.

I came first, spewing come all over the couch. Ronnie came a few strokes later, driving into me one last time and holding my hips tight as he fired his wad deep inside me.

We stood like that for a moment, taking in the view of the city, a view we weren't likely to see again for a long time, until we caught our breath.

Then Ronnie pulled away, retrieved his robe, and called room service for another bottle of champagne so we could drink ourselves to sleep.

The next day we returned to the road, to one-night-stands with pick-up bands, to hustling T-shirts and CDs to die-hard fans, and to fucking each other in cheap motels after every show.

Ronnie still has his dream, and I'm living mine.

Thank God for rock 'n' roll.

TOTAL PACKAGE

Political correctness hadn't reached my part of Texas back then and the locals still referred to me as a mailman. As a substitute letter carrier, I covered rural routes on a rotating basis, a different one each day when the regular carriers had their days off. Saturdays I ran RR#2 southwest of town, puttering along the shoulder in a right-hand drive Jeep that had seen better days, stopping every so often to fill roadside mailboxes with bills and bulk mail.

I knew more about the people on my routes than they realized. Five-foot-two, two-hundred-and-fifty-pound Ethel May Raditz told everyone she was on a diet but received a package nearly every week from Godiva. Tom Jobe seemed to be preparing for the apocalypse because he subscribed to a dozen survivalist magazines. And Vince DiMarco, at that time the newest stop on the route, had something to hide because he received more than the usual amount of mail in plain brown wrappers.

He wasn't the only one around town with something to hide. I was so deep in the closet I wasn't sure I would ever find my way out. I'd suspected I was different in high school because I snuck glances at the other guys when we showered and had no interest at all in the girls—even after Billy Roy Johnson found a way to sneak peeks into their locker room through a hole in the wall of the equipment room—but I'd never told anyone about my proclivity, and I had certainly not done anything about it at the time. Not where I lived. Not in rural Texas.

My family didn't have the money to send me off to college, so I worked various jobs around town until I got on with the USPS. Once I had a steady income, I rented a small house three blocks from the station and proceeded to lead a double life. Derek to my family, Rick to most everyone else, I shot pool with my friends at Gully's on Saturday nights, attended the Methodist church Sunday mornings, and spent all the holidays with my family.

Sexually frustrated because I wasn't interested in the available women my age—most of whom had been through at least one marriage and were either available to every man who bought them a drink or were seeking baby daddies—I sought release during occasional trips away from town. Dallas and Austin became my favorite travel destinations, but after a few years of casual encounters with men who had no interest in sharing phone numbers or last names, I resigned myself to the probability that I would never experience the kind of relationship that my parents—married thirty-five years and showing no signs of wear—enjoyed.

As much as I desired sexual congress with a hard-bodied young man, I wanted something more. I wanted a relationship measured in years and months, not hours and minutes. I wanted the total package. And I despaired of ever finding it.

One Saturday morning, about two months after he moved into the old Denton place, I found myself with a plain brown envelope addressed to Vince DiMarco that had been stamped with a postage due notification. I knew most of the people on my route—I'd gone to school with them or their kin, worshipped in church beside them, or was related to them in some way—so I usually left postage-due mail in their boxes. Charlie Waterson, the carrier who worked Monday through Friday, would find the appropriate amount of money waiting in the mailboxes the next delivery day. But I didn't know Vince. I'd never met him—had never even seen him—and the only things I knew about him, other than what I could discern from casual glances at his mail, was what my second cousin Sally Jo, the real estate agent who'd sold him the old Denton place, had told the family during one of our occasional Sunday afternoon cookouts. He was handsome, single, and worked out of Waco as a claims adjuster for an insurance company.

I glanced at my watch. I was ahead of schedule and nosey, so I eased the Jeep past Vince's roadside mailbox, turned up the short drive, and stopped behind a recent-model Lexus. After killing the engine, I unfolded myself from the Jeep, walked past the Lexus and up the steps to the porch, and leaned on the bell. I heard it clang somewhere deep inside the house. I waited a few minutes and then I leaned on it again.

Just as I was getting ready to leave a pink form telling

Vince when he could collect his postage-due envelope from the post office in town, he opened the front door. Wet, ripped, and wearing nothing but a royal blue towel wrapped loosely around his hips, he seemed as surprised by me as I was by him.

His gaze quickly traveled from my white pith helmet down over my blue short-sleeve sport-style knit shirt with the U.S. Mail emblem above the left breast pocket, over my navy-blue shorts—worn the regulation three inches above midknee—with the dark blue stripe on the outside seam, over my calf-length blue-gray socks with two navy rings at the top, on down to my polished black work shoes, and then back up to my eyes. Unlike many of my coworkers, I looked good in my regulation uniform. I groomed myself appropriately, took care of my body, bought uniforms that fit, and cared for them as well as I cared for my street clothes.

"I'm sorry," he said, apologizing for his appearance. "You caught me in the Jacuzzi."

I held up the heavy envelope. "This came postage due—"

A black-and-white Border collie shot out the door and grabbed the envelope. My free hand instinctively reached for my pepper spray before I realized the dog wasn't attacking me; it was attacking the plain brown envelope and whatever was inside. For a moment we played tug-of-war with it. Then the envelope tore open, and its contents fell to the porch, revealing a familiar magazine, one that I received at my post office box two towns north of the town where I actually lived.

"No, Elroy, no!"

Vince grabbed the dog's collar and wrestled it back into the house as I bent to retrieve the magazine. As he struggled with the dog, Vince's towel dropped to the floor. He wore nothing beneath it, and I found myself eye-to-thigh with his muscular legs. His thick phallus and heavy scrotum hung mere inches from my face. If he had experienced any shrinkage from his time in the Jacuzzi, it wasn't evident.

I licked my lips and slowly straightened up with the magazine in my hand, unexpected desire flooding through my entire body.

Vince, still struggling to control the Border collie, made no effort to cover himself. He asked, "How much do I owe?"

I told him.

"I'll get it. Wait here."

He pulled the dog back and closed the door, which pushed the wet blue towel onto the porch at my feet. I nudged it with the toe of one black shoe, wondering if I should pick it up. I decided instead to step away from the door, and I waited on the edge of the porch near the steps.

When Vince reappeared, he wore chinos and a pale green polo shirt that hugged his thick chest and trim waist. He stepped onto the porch and closed the door behind him to prevent the Border collie from darting out again.

He handed me the appropriate amount of change.

I handed him the magazine.

As he took it from my outstretched hand, our fingers touched. The warmth spreading through me turned into a raging fire. I felt myself stir within my uniform shorts. I said, "I—"

"Yes?" He waited expectantly for me to continue.

My throat was dry, so I swallowed hard and tried again. "I subscribe to the same publication. I—"

Vince looked at me, his dark eyes narrowing as if seeing me for the first time. He cocked his head to one side. "Really?"

I wet my lips. "I rented a post office box a couple of towns over so no one around here would know."

"You haven't told anyone?"

"Not even my family."

"So why tell me?"

I motioned toward the magazine he now held.

"Because of this?"

I nodded. Had I made a mistake? Had I jumped to a mistaken conclusion? "I need to get back on the road," I told him. "I have lots of mail to deliver."

As I turned to go, he stopped me.

"How about dinner?" Vince suggested. "I was going to grill, and it'll be no trouble to throw on another steak and couple more ears of corn."

A date? He was asking me on a date? I had planned to drink beer and shoot pool at Gully's with my friends—my clueless friends—that evening, just like I did most Saturday nights. We certainly couldn't go anywhere in town.

"Maybe you can join me in the Jacuzzi after," he continued. "You don't need a suit, and I have a towel big enough for two."

"I—" I hesitated while my mind raced in a dozen different directions at once. I had always sought companionship outside of town. Did I dare take advantage of an opportunity that came to me? Did I dare risk the possibility that someone might see my car parked in front of Vince's later that evening and question why I was spending time with an outsider? I did.

I asked, "What time?"

I returned to Vince's house that evening. I had changed from my uniform into a form-fitting polo shirt, skin-tight Wrangler jeans starched and ironed to put razor-sharp creases down the legs, and well-worn, but not worn-out ropers. Vince wore a light blue, short-sleeve seersucker shirt; tan-colored, pleated-front chino shorts, and slip-on deck shoes without socks. It couldn't have been more obvious that this was a case of country boy meets city boy.

My host led me through the house. I had not been in the place while the Dentons had owned it, but I suspected the interior had never looked so good. The white walls had been recently painted, the hardwood floors had been polished to a shine, and the furniture was sparse but tasteful. Elroy spotted me as soon as we stepped onto the back porch, but the Border collie didn't seem nearly as interested in me as he had been when I was standing on the front porch in my uniform.

"I hope you don't think I've gone overboard," Vince said, "but you're the first guest I've had since moving in."

He had gone overboard. In the center of the patio sat

a glass-topped, wrought iron patio table that had been set for two, with expensive china and real silver. I said, "Maybe a little."

Vince opened a bottle of red wine and poured a glass for each of us. Then he slapped a pair of T-bones and four ears of corn still in their husks on the propane grill and closed the lid. I sipped the wine politely, adjusting my beer-trained palate to the unfamiliar taste.

We made small talk while the steaks cooked, discussing the weather more than anything else, and before I realized how much time had passed, Vince was pulling the steaks and the corn off the grill and preparing our plates.

I sat, he sat, and then we stared at each other.

After a moment of awkward silence, I blurted, "I don't know what to do. I've never done this before."

Vince's eyes widened in surprise. "Never?"

I realized he had misunderstood me, so I quickly explained. "I'm not a virgin," I said. "That's not what I meant. I meant I've never done this." I indicated the dinner table with a sweep of one hand. "I've never had a date."

He smiled. "All we have to do is eat."

"I can do that," I said with a smile. "I've been doing that my entire life." Then, between bites, I told him about my trips to Dallas and Austin without providing intimate details.

"And why did you find those trips so unfulfilling?"

I explained about my parents and how I'd always

wanted the kind of relationship they had and how I despaired of ever finding it in rural Texas.

"You can search the world over and not find your soul mate," Vince said, "or you can step out your front door and stumble over him."

Is that what had happened?

"What about you?" I asked. "Have you ever—?"

"I was in a relationship for about a year," Vince explained. "I thought he was the one, but I was wrong. Horribly wrong. I had to get as far away from him as I could without changing jobs, and that's why I moved here."

"Is he still in Waco?"

"As far as I know, but there's little chance our paths will cross."

Vince grilled bananas in their skins for dessert, halving them lengthwise and covering the warm fruit with brown sugar and cinnamon after removing them from the grill. We used spoons to scoop the bananas from the skins and before long we were laughing and feeding each other.

After we finished dessert, Vince tossed one of the steak bones to Elroy and then I helped him clear the table and carry the dishes into the kitchen.

I don't know how to explain it—maybe it was the wine, maybe it was the full belly—but I felt comfortable with Vince, so comfortable that we spent the better part of the evening draining a second bottle of wine and telling each other our life stories. He had been out of the closet since his sophomore year of college, and I had yet to tell any of my family or friends about my secret life.

"Someday you will," Vince said, "and when you do, no matter what their reaction, it will lift a huge burden from you."

A few minutes before midnight, the second bottle of wine long emptied and the buzz mostly worn off, I excused myself, telling my host that I had church in the morning.

Vince walked me to the front door and opened it. As I hesitated in the open doorway, he told me how much he had enjoyed our evening together. Then he took my face between his hands and covered my lips with his. Surprised but not a bit hesitant, I returned his kiss with equal fervor. As we kissed, my body quivered with desire.

When the kiss ended, Vince stepped back and said, "You'd best leave now before we do something we might regret later."

As I drove away, my jeans so tight at my crotch that I thought the zipper might burst from the pressure, I realized Vince and I had not used the Jacuzzi or his towel big enough for two.

That's how our relationship began, and we spent our next several dates revealing our souls and not our scrotums. In fact, I didn't see Vince naked again until our fifth date, when we ended the evening asleep in each other's arms. By then I knew I had found someone special.

I had found my total package.

HEART ON

The scrubs worn by the staff and the average age of the people using the exercise equipment made the medical center's cardiopulmonary rehabilitation center nothing but a high-priced gym with short-term memberships paid for by various health insurance plans. In my early fifties, I was younger than most of the other patients, but that didn't make me any healthier. Only a few weeks earlier, after decades of inadequate exercise and poor dietary habits, I had undergone quadruple heart-bypass surgery. Following surgery my cardiologist had prescribed—in fact, had demanded—my participation in rehab.

Other than the occasional use of hotel fitness centers while traveling for business, I had not been inside a gym of any kind since college, so when I first shuffled in, I was unprepared for the number and variety of fitness machines filling the rehab center. Treadmills lined one wall; stationary and recumbent bicycles lined another, and arranged throughout the remaining space in some pattern that I could not fathom were various weight machines and equipment that I could not identify at first glance.

The physical therapist assigned to my case—a hot little number in his mid-thirties who would have made my cock rise under other circumstances—took me into a private room where he weighed me, measured me and discussed my cardiologist's rehabilitation plan. As we talked, he attached a trio of electrodes to my chest, sticking them where my hair was only beginning to regrow. Wires from the electrodes trailed under my shirt to a transmitter that hung from my belt and sent data about my heart to an EKG at the nurse's station in the center of the outer equipment room.

Then he led me out of the private room, stuck me on a treadmill set to the slowest speed and walked away. I could barely keep up and I stopped the treadmill after a few minutes.

Trevor noticed my distress and hurried to my side. He helped me to a nearby chair. "You're already out of breath."

"You," I said with a wink, "take my breath away."

He laughed and patted my hand. "You're in no condition to make passes, Mr. Tate."

"Call me Bob," I said. "And if I was?"

When he leaned forward and whispered in my ear, my physical therapist provided a workout incentive that I had not anticipated when I'd shuffled into the rehab center an hour earlier. "I'd fuck you so hard your heart would break the EKG."

"Is that a promise?"

"Get well," Trevor said as he straightened, "and we'll see what happens."

An elderly woman was struggling on one of the stationary bicycles in the outer room, so Trevor left me sitting in the chair while he attended to her needs. I watched him work with the woman. Even the loose-fitting blue scrubs couldn't hide the classic V of his figure—broad shoulders, thick chest, narrow waist, and tight ass held aloft on muscular legs—nor could it hide the tantalizing bulge of his personal exercise equipment.

I remembered when just the thought of unwrapping the package of a man like Trevor would have given me serious wood and weeks of masturbation fantasies, but as I sat watching him work with the woman my cock didn't even twitch once. I had not noticed any significant diminishing of sexual performance prior to heart surgery, so I didn't know if the lack of response to Trevor's sex appeal was a cardiovascular problem or a side-effect of all the drugs pumping through my body.

Trevor was back at my side before I had time to overthink the cause of my dangling dick. With his help, I returned to the treadmill for a few minutes more, but I didn't do much else during my first visit to the rehab center.

"I want you to strut out of here when you finish rehab," Trevor said during my second visit as he attached the electrodes to my chest before my workout, "looking and feeling better than you have in years."

Though his fingers did not linger, and he didn't act in any way that might be considered unprofessional, I appreciated Trevor's touch. My previous relationship had ended almost a year before my surgery and the last two men to touch my chest had been the one who broke my heart and the one who cracked my chest to put it back together. "I bet you say that to all your patients."

"Of course, I do," he said, "but with you I mean it. Take a look around. With most of these people I'm just trying to ensure they can take care of themselves when their insurance benefits expire. I'm expecting something more from you."

"A broken EKG?"

He smiled as he switched on the transmitter hanging from my belt. "But not today."

I had not considered myself out of shape prior to my surgery, but clearly, I was. The purpose of rehab was to increase both my stamina and my strength, and I spent most of my first few visits shuffling along on the treadmill. Then Trevor started me on the weight machines and gave me exercises I could do at home with two-pound free weights. Over the next few visits, when he wasn't flirting with me, he slowly increased the treadmill speed and the treadmill incline, just as he slowly increased the weight, I lifted on the weight machines. After several weeks I realized that my body had changed and was still changing. Not only was I able to walk longer distances at higher speeds without losing my breath, my pants were looser and my sleeves tighter around my biceps. Though my weight barely changed, fat was morphing into muscle.

Just as important—to me, at least—my cardiologist weaned me from several of the drugs I'd been taking. The combination of frequent exercise and diminished chemical side effects rejuvenated my cardiovascular system, and during the last few weeks of rehab my cock responded whenever Trevor touched me or I had impure thoughts about him. Twice during the last week of rehab, I awoke in the middle of the night while dreaming about my physical therapist, surprised when I attempted to roll over and found my progress impeded by an erection as firm as any I'd had presurgery.

"Ready for graduation?" Trevor asked when I finished my last scheduled workout. By then I had—at least once during the previous weeks—lifted, pulled, pushed, pressed, squeezed, spun or walked on every piece of exercise equipment in the rehabilitation center gym. At home I had moved up from two-pound free weights to fifteen-pound free weights, and I had returned to work with no restrictions on my activities.

Trevor led me into the same private room we'd used when I had shuffled in for my first day of rehab. After I sat on the stool, he had me remove my shirt and again he measured everything. Three inches had disappeared from my waist and my biceps were three quarters of an inch bigger around. I hadn't believed it was possible, but I was in better shape than when I had arrived. Even my chest hair had regrown, obscuring the ten-inch scar bisecting my chest.

"You've made a lot of progress," Trevor said. He sat on a stool several inches shorter than mine, facing me with his left hand resting on my leg, just above my knee. "It's amazing what you can do now that you couldn't do when you first shuffled in here."

"You wouldn't believe what I'm capable of now." I stared straight into his pale-blue eyes as I reached out and placed my hand on top of his.

He glanced down at our hands but didn't pull his away. When his gaze again met mine, he asked, "Are you healthy enough for private therapy sessions?"

"My doctor seems to think so."

"You realize your insurance doesn't cover private therapy."

I smiled. "What are you suggesting?"

The vertical scar indicating where the surgeon had entered my chest was no longer the angry red welt it had been, but it was still sensitive to the touch. Trevor pressed the tip of his index finger to the top of the scar and traced its length down between the wires still attached to the electrodes stuck to my chest, causing me to shiver. No one had ever touched my scar like that, and it was a more intimate act than any other he could have done. My cock reacted immediately, tightening my pants.

"You're not my patient anymore," he said.

"What does that mean?"

"It means I can do this." He leaned forward and lightly pressed his lips against mine. After he drew back, he searched for any sign that I might have been offended or taken aback by his action. When he saw none, he continued. "You can't stop exercising just because it's no longer covered by your insurance. You'll need to join a gym or find some other way to continue the work we've done here."

"But who will ensure that I'm on the right track?"

"I can continue to do that for you," he said. He lowered his voice and leaned forward. "I even know a few exercises we can do in private."

"You'd be willing to do that?"

His left hand slid up my thigh until it stopped less than an inch from my rapidly swelling cock.

I glanced at the door. "Someone might interrupt us."

"Don't worry," he said. "The door's locked."

Trevor undid my belt buckle, unbuttoned my jeans and slid my zipper down. I lifted my buttocks so he could slide my pants down, and when he did the transmitter still hanging from my belt clunked against the stool. I barely noticed the sound and didn't think about it as Trevor reached inside my boxers and wrapped his hand around the base of my cock, capturing some of my untamed pubic hair in his fist.

"I'm surprised it's so hard," I said. "I haven't been exercising it recently."

"Well, it seems to be up for a little physical therapy." Trevor watched my eyes as he stroked upward until his encircling thumb and forefinger reached the helmet head of my cock. Then he stroked back to the base.

He repeated the motion several times until a bead of pre-come glistened atop the tiny slit. Then he leaned forward, took the head of my cock in his mouth and locked his lips around my glans. He licked away the drop of pre-come and spanked my cock head with his tongue as he tightened his fist around the shaft and pumped hard and fast.

My heart began to beat hard, and I gripped the stool with both hands to keep from scooting off it as I thrust my hips forward and back in rhythm to the pumping of Trevor's fist. My balls began to tighten, and my cock grew even stiffer. I knew I was about to come, and I couldn't have stopped myself even if I had wanted to. I didn't know how thick the walls were or how well the door sealed in sounds, so I bit my bottom lip to keep from crying out.

I came hard, so hard I jerked involuntarily. I might have fallen if there hadn't been a wall only a few inches behind me that kept me from going backward off the stool. The sudden change in my position caused my pants to slip from my thighs, taking the transmitter with them down to my ankles and pulling the trio of electrodes from my chest.

My cock throbbed inside Trevor's mouth as I fired warm come against the back of his throat. He swallowed and swallowed again, holding my cock in his mouth until he had sucked it dry. Then he drew away, leaned back and looked up at me.

"You," I said, repeating what I had told him the first time he'd put me on the treadmill, "take my breath away."

I slipped from the stool, tucked my semierect cock into my boxers, and put my clothes in order. Trevor took the transmitter from me, grabbed the clipboard with my paperwork and opened the door. Then he walked me to the nurse's station and looked at the report generated by the EKG. He looked up at me. "You didn't break it."

I lowered my voice as I leaned across the desk. "That thing was recording?"

"Until it fell off," he said as he tapped the report. "I'm no doctor, but I think your heart's made a remarkable recovery."

"Not a complete recovery," I said. I told him about the man who had broken my heart almost a year before my surgery.

"No surgery will cure that," he said.

"But continued exercise with the right partner will." I invited him to dinner the following Friday.

Trevor came directly from work, still wearing his blue scrubs. I greeted him with a kiss and led him into the kitchen where I was preparing boneless pork chops with an orange marmalade sauce, had au gratin potatoes in the oven and a spinach salad in the fridge. I handed him a bottle of wine to open and soon we were flirting, sipping wine and watching the pork chops brown.

"Have you found a gym?"

"Not yet," I admitted. "I really haven't looked."

"You should start," he said as he touched my bicep. "You don't want all our hard work to disappear."

I also didn't want lectures from my cardiologist, who had been quite impressed by the amount of progress I had made in such a short time, thanks to the exercise routine Trevor put me through. "I'll start tomorrow," I said. "Tonight, though, you promised to show me a few exercises we can do in private."

He placed his wineglass on the kitchen counter and then captured my face between his hands. He covered my lips with his and kissed me long, deep and hard. I wanted to wrap my arms around Trevor and pull him close, but I held tongs in one hand, my wineglass in the other, and couldn't reach the counter to put them down. That didn't stop my tongue from meeting his and engaging in a fiery dance of desire.

The kiss didn't end until my knees grew rubbery, and I felt as weak as I had the first day Trevor put me on a treadmill. He drew back, picked up his wine glass and said, "That's just the warm-up. Wait 'til we get to the stretching exercises."

I wanted to rush through dinner, but I didn't dare. Once I confirmed that the potatoes were done and the chops were perfect, I served dinner in the dining room. As we ate, we talked, laughed, flirted and drank our way through the bottle of wine.

We didn't bother clearing the table when we finished. I took Trevor's hand and led him into the bedroom where I had already turned down the sheets, had a fresh tube of lube on the nightstand, and had been burning a vanilla-scented candle since midafternoon.

We peeled off our clothes, tossing them aside without care. When we were both naked, I took a moment to appreciate Trevor's sculpted body, which was even better than I had imagined it, before I grabbed his ass and pulled him to me. Our cocks collided, shifted, and then my cock pressed his abdomen and his pressed against mine.

I covered his mouth with mine and shoved my tongue

between his lips, tasting orange marmalade and wine when our tongues met. He slipped one hand between us, wrapped his fist around my cock and began tugging at it. I didn't want to come too soon, so I pushed his hand away.

Trevor ended our kiss by pulling away and turning his back. He grabbed the lube, twisted off the top and handed the tube to me. As I slathered a good bit of it up and down the length of my cock, Trevor bent over the bed, braced his knees against the mattress and thrust his ass up at me. I squeezed a good dollop of lube into his ass crack and then used my fingers to massage the tight pucker of his ass hole. Soon it opened to one lube-slickened finger and I pistoned my finger in and out. When he seemed relaxed, I pulled my finger free and pressed the head of my cock against Trevor's ass hole.

I don't know if he was quite ready, but I pressed forward anyhow, driving my slickened cock deep into him as he cried out. I drew back until only my cock head remained inside him, and then drove forward again.

As I fucked the physical therapist, I held tight to one of his hips and reached around him with my free hand. After I wrapped my lube-slickened fist around his stiff cock, I began pumping up and down the length of his shaft, my hand not quite in rhythm with my hips.

The closer I came to orgasm, the faster I pumped into Trevor's ass and the faster my hand stroked his cock. He came first, firing a glob of come onto the sheets and covering my fist with his sexual effluent.

I released my grip on his cock, even though he was still coming, and grabbed his other hip. I slammed into him another dozen times, each thrust harder and faster than the one before it.

And then I came.

I came hard, emptying my balls inside his ass as I pressed myself tight against him. My heart beat wildly inside my chest and for a moment I worried that I had overexerted myself. Even as I thought that, I knew that I didn't care.

When I caught my breath and my cock finally stopped spasming in Trevor's ass, I pulled away and flopped onto the bed, barely missing the wet spot he'd created. He climbed into bed beside me.

"Think that would have broken the EKG?" I asked.

"I'm sure of it," he said, out of breath. "It almost broke me."

Trevor spent the night, and the next morning we fucked again. I expected him to leave after I prepared breakfast and we cleaned the dishes from the night before, but he had another idea.

"You're not going to find a gym if I leave you to your own devices," he said, "so get dressed and come with me."

I did as instructed, and soon we were walking into a gym not far from the cardiopulmonary rehabilitation center, one where the men at the workout machines were serious about their workouts. The place smelled of sweat and testosterone and the men were dressed in sweats and sleeveless T-shirts. The only music came from the clanking of weights and the grunting of men lifting.

At Trevor's insistence, I joined the gym that day, and when we aren't working out together in my bedroom, we're working out together at the gym he made me join.

I'm now more buff than I've ever been, I've rebuffed the advances of several of the gym's other members and my cardiologist gets happier each time I have a checkup.

Surgery may have repaired my damaged heart, but my physical therapist repaired my broken heart.

HONEY DO ME

After I stepped out of the shower, I opened my bathroom window blinds and found myself staring at powerful arms reaching upward, broad shoulders, thick chest tapering to a slim waist, six-pack abs, and all of it covered with a glistening sheen of perspiration.

Then I took in the rest of the picture. The gorgeous hunk of a man outside my window was standing on a stepladder and the next thing that caught my eye was the bulging package barely restrained by his tight-fitting Levi's. I let my gaze climb upward to his square chin, pale blue eyes, and sandy hair worn in a freshly cut flattop.

He smiled when he saw me staring at him.

I pushed the window open. "What the hell are you doing?"

"Sorry," he said as he lowered his arms. His deep voice carried a hint of gravel. "I didn't realize anyone was home."

I repeated my question.

"Repairing the gutters."

"Who asked you to do that?"

"I have a work order from the owner," he said. "I can get it if you want."

"*I'm* the owner," I said, "and I haven't ordered anything."

The man outside my bathroom window climbed down the stepladder and headed toward the white panel van parked at the curb while I headed toward the front door. I was halfway there before I realized I still held my bath towel in my hand, and I wondered how much of my still-wet body had been visible through the window.

I wrapped the towel around my waist before opening the front door and pushing open the screen. I met the handsome handyman on my front porch, he handed me a clipboard with a work order clipped to it, and I saw the problem right away. The work order was for 1202 Elm, and I live at 1220 Elm.

The handyman stood almost four inches taller than me, so I looked up at him to ask, "Are you dyslexic?"

"No, why?"

I spun the clipboard around and pointed to his error.

"Tell you what," he said. "I'm almost done here. Why don't you just let me finish—no charge—and then I'll head down the street."

My gutters had been sagging for years, despite my best intentions to have them seen to, so I agreed. Then I asked, "What else do you do?"

"A little of everything," he said. "No plumbing or electrical work, nothing that requires certification or a special license, but everything else you might put on the 'honey-do' list for the man of the house."

At that moment, as I stared at the hunk standing before me, my list only contained one entry: *Honey, do me.*

At the thought of seeing the handsome handyman sans jeans, my cock began to swell, threatening to tent the front of the towel wrapped around my waist. I quickly handed back the clipboard and said, "Why don't you come back after you finish with 1202? I might have something else for you to do."

"How about later this afternoon?" he countered. He peeled a bent business card out of his back pocket and handed it to me. I could tell he'd printed it off his computer because I could feel the rough edges where one business card had been separated from another. I glanced at it—*Handy Andy,* a website address, and a phone number—while he continued. "I have three more jobs lined up for today and I'm already behind schedule. I can be back around five."

Dinnertime.

I said, "That's fine."

While I toweled dry and dressed, he finished repairing my gutters and then drove down the street to the correct address. I spent the morning and most of the afternoon shopping with Riz, a longtime friend with a fashion sense similar to mine, and purchased a variety of new clothes in celebration of the end of a six-month diet and exercise plan that had done wonders for my figure. Over mid-afternoon lattes I told him about the man I'd found outside my bathroom window.

"Honey," he said as he placed one hand on my forearm, "you just have all the luck. The only thing I ever see when I look out my windows is a brick wall." Riz lives in a fifth-floor apartment and all the windows face a wall on the far side of the alley. He doesn't live there for the view; he lives there because the rent is dirt-cheap.

"He's returning at five."

Riz patted my forearm. "See, all the luck."

"What should I do?"

"I know what I would do if a man like the one you described was coming to my apartment at dinner time."

"What?"

He told me, in quite graphic detail, and I had to wait twenty minutes after Riz finished before I could slide out of the booth without displaying a bulge in my chinos.

I had dinner ready when Handy Andy rang my doorbell at three minutes past five. I hadn't had time to visit the hair stylist, but I had managed to shower, shave, manscape, and slip into new chinos that better fit my slimmed-down figure and a new shirt that brought out the color of my eyes.

When I opened the door with a silver pasta server in my hand and stared at him through the screen, I was surprised to see that my guest had also found time to clean up. He had replaced his faded jeans and bare chest for Levi's so crisply pressed the creases could have sliced bread and a sky-blue polo shirt that hugged his chest like a second skin.

He mistook my surprise at his appearance for surprise at his presence and reminded me, "You asked me to return when I finished for the day. You said you might have work for me."

"I did, didn't I?" I motioned toward the kitchen with the pasta server. "You've caught me at a bad time. I was about to sit down to dinner."

"That's okay. I can come back another time."

I hesitated as if I hadn't planned what I would say next and it had just come to me. "Have you eaten?"

"No, I—"

"Then why don't you join me?" I offered. "It's nothing special—spaghetti with meatballs, garlic bread, a bottle of Chianti—" I let the offer hang in the air.

"I could do that," he said. "In fact, I think I'd like that."

I pushed open the screen and welcomed Andy to my house.

"Andrew," he corrected. "Andy's just for business because Handy Andrew doesn't roll of the tongue."

I laughed appropriately, told him to call me Lon, and led him to the kitchen. I hadn't yet set the dining room table, so I put my dinner guest to work preparing the table while I finished preparing the meal.

Soon we were seated at the dining room table, our plates loaded with spaghetti, our wine glasses filled with Chianti, and hearty hunks of garlic bread within reach. We didn't talk much, at first. Andrew complimented me on the spaghetti sauce, but I demurred because Riz had provided the recipe and I'd slavishly followed his directions. Then I asked how Andrew had come to be self-employed, and he told me that he'd been in the Army but that somebody had asked and he'd told. Rather than explain his discharge to potential employers, he'd used his savings to buy a van, a cell phone, a Yellow Pages ad, and a simple website.

"I slept on my brother's couch for two years before I was making enough to get my own place," he said as he sopped spaghetti sauce off his plate with the last hunk of bread, "but I'm doing pretty good these days."

I could only imagine how well his business was doing with the military base nearby and all the families forced to make do with one parent—usually the husband—stationed overseas.

Andrew popped the last hunk of bread in his mouth, leaving a spot of sauce below his bottom lip. Without thinking, I reached out and wiped it away with the ball of my thumb. As I stuck the ball of my thumb between my lips and licked away the sauce, Andrew asked, "You don't really have any work for me, do you?"

I had to admit that I didn't.

"So, you invited me back for this?" He nodded at the empty plates.

"I hadn't planned that far in advance," I admitted. "I just wanted to see more of you."

"I would have thought you'd seen quite enough of me through the window." He smiled. "I know I saw quite a bit of you."

He'd looked.

I'd thought he had.

"And?"

He smiled. "And I liked what I saw."

Almost two years had passed since any man—Riz didn't count—had complimented my appearance. Suddenly nervous, I stood and grabbed our plates. "Help me clear the table."

I hurried into the kitchen, filled the sink with soapy water, and began washing the dishes that Andrew carried to me. I'd left the kitchen a mess, so I had more to wash than just what we'd used at the table. I was just beginning to scrub the cookware when Andrew stepped up behind me, trapping me against the sink, and put one hand on each of my biceps.

His hands were big, his fingers long, his grip firm, and I felt my heart skip a beat. Then he kissed the back of my neck and I let out a contented sigh. I stopped scrubbing the pot and turned my head. He kissed my ear and my cheek. He covered my mouth with his but kept me trapped against the sink so that I could not turn to face him, and I felt his turgid cock through the fabric of our clothes as he pressed against me.

He pulled my shirttail free of my chinos and unbuttoned my shirt, slid his big hands up my chest and over my pecs. Six months earlier—and two of the reasons for my self-imposed diet and exercise plan—I'd had man-boobs. Riz had even threatened to take me to Victoria's Secret to be fitted for a manssiere. But now my pecs were firm in Andrew's hands and my nipples grew hard as he thumbed them.

His hands slid down my chest and over my now-firm

abdomen. Then he unbuckled my belt, unfastened my chinos, and dropped them to the floor. By the time my silk boxers followed, my cock was fully and painfully erect. He wrapped one hand around it and pumped his fist up and down. I'd always thought I was better equipped than average, but my cock felt small in his big hand.

Andrew continued kissing my neck as he slowly stroked me, and before long I couldn't restrain myself. My breath caught in the back of my throat. I came on his hand and on the counter.

He held my cock until it stopped spasming and I started breathing again. Then he half-stepped backward and I heard his pants hit the floor behind me.

I'd used half a stick of butter to make the garlic bread and I'd left the other half on the counter. It's a good thing I'm not lactose intolerant because Andrew grabbed it and buttered me up with his fingers before he slipped his erect cock between my buns.

He slid his thick cock along the length of my ass crack but that wasn't what I wanted at all. I rose on my tiptoes and Andrew shifted position so that his cock head pressed against my sphincter. My orgasm had relaxed me, the butter had made me slick, and Andrew's cock was deep inside me in one smooth motion.

Andrew held my hips as he drew back and pushed forward, churning butter as his pumping motion steadily gained speed. I was still trapped against the sink and my flaccid cock slapped against the counter every time the handyman drove into me.

I started pushing back against him, thrusting my ass

backward each time Andrew drove forward, meeting each of his powerful thrusts with my own.

Then, without any warning at all, he slammed into me one last time, shuddered, and fired hot spunk deep inside my ass. He leaned against me, catching his breath until his cock finished spasming, before pulling away.

I turned and we stared at each other without speaking. We were half undressed, surrounded by pots and pans that still needed to be washed, and I realized that my diet and exercise plan had made me desirable again.

I reached out for Andrews's hand and, after we both stepped out of the clothing pooled around our ankles, I led him to the bedroom.

"And then what?" Riz asked. We were having lunch together at a sandwich shop near his apartment.

I smiled. "Let's just say I didn't finish cleaning the kitchen until after breakfast."

Riz placed his hand on my forearm and said with a wink, "You know, I need my gutters fixed. What's Handy Andy's number?"

"You live in an apartment," I said. Then I realized what he meant and pulled my arm away. "You find your own handyman. Andrew's mine."

YOUNG MAN'S GAME

I relied on my good looks to get me everything I ever wanted when I was in my twenties, traveling to photo shoots on six of the seven continents and enjoying commitment-free sex with other models and the men attracted to us, but my modeling career abandon me when makeup artists started taking longer to prep me than photographers took to capture my image.

When the top fashion houses no longer requested me by name, my agent promoted a receptionist to junior agent and made me his first client. The afternoon Delray called to inform me, in his chipmunk-chipper voice, that he was now representing me and that he had booked a one-day shoot for a hemorrhoid cream, I told him he could shove the gig up the same orifice where he might apply that cream, and I quit the business.

Unlike many of my contemporaries—boys who became men in a make-believe world where natural beauty and easy money lead to over-indulgence in multiple vices—I had never required rehab to control my urges, nor had I become intimate friends with plastic surgeons in a vain attempt to recapture the youthful appearance that was so obviously escaping me.

I sold my condo in New York City, emptied my bank accounts, and returned home to my family's West Texas cattle ranch, a place that favored hard work over good looks, and during the next two decades I put on forty pounds of muscle and saw the lines on my face that makeup artists had tried to spackle over develop into deep crags. The sun and the wind turned my exposed skin to leather and a farmer's tan—face, neck, and the lower three-quarters of my arms—replaced the carefully cultivated all-over tan I once had.

The one thing I hadn't counted on when I returned home was the dearth of potential sexual partners so far from any town large enough to have a stoplight. With only three places to meet people at the town nearest the family ranch—a diner, a feed store, and a Methodist church—I resigned myself to taking my sex life in my own hands. And for too many years I did exactly that.

Fifty was safely in my rearview when my past caught up to me.

I spent the morning at the feed store, talking to Carl about an increase in our monthly order of mineral supplements, and stopped at the town's only diner for lunch before heading back to the ranch. I was sitting at the counter, halfway through a chicken-fried steak, pinto beans, and double-order of creamed potatoes, when a stranger left the booth in which he'd been sitting and straddled the stool beside me.

"May I take your picture?"

The first time I'd heard that line I'd been sitting at the other end of the counter fresh out of high school and two months away from starting classes at Texas A&M over in College Station, following in the bootsteps of my older brothers. I'd thought the sweating fat man asking the question was hitting on me, but he turned out to be a talent scout who'd taken a wrong turn on his way from Ft. Worth to Amarillo and had driven too far south. A month later I had an agent, my first modeling gigs, and an anemic photographer's assistant giving me blowjobs.

I examined the handsome man sitting beside me and felt my cock rearrange itself in my jeans. Almost ten years my junior, he was slender like someone who watched his weight but was unaccustomed to hard, physical labor. He dressed like a catalog cowboy, though, not like a cattleman, in a blue and black embroidered western snap-front shirt, too-new Levi's jeans, and high-heeled ostrich Justin boots that showed no sign of wear. A black felt Stetson remained on the table he'd just vacated. His dark hair was slicked back, and he didn't have hat hair, as if he carried the Stetson rather than wore it. Wherever he was from, he clearly wasn't from West Texas.

I asked, "Why?"

He pulled a business card from his shirt pocket and placed it on the counter next to my plate. "I'm a photographer," he explained as I glanced at the card and learned that Steve Carson hailed from Austin, the liberal center of the conservative state where we lived. "I'm shooting pictures for a coffee table book called *Contemporary Cowboys* and—"

"No, thanks," I told him. I turned away and forked another bite of chicken-fried steak. I dredged it through the creamed potatoes and white gravy and stuck it in my mouth.

The photographer touched my arm, sending an unexpected jolt of sexual electricity through my body that caused my balls to tighten. I turned toward him.

"You're exactly the type of man I've been looking for," he explained. "You look the part and everything."

I wore a blue denim shirt with the cuffs rolled halfway up my forearms, faded Wrangler jeans molded to my lower anatomy, and cow flop-colored ropers—low-heeled cowboy boots—with unevenly worn soles caused by a slightly bow-legged gait that came from years astride a quarter horse. Unlike the photographer beside me, my apparel wasn't some wanna-be Marlboro Man garb ordered off the Internet, but the daily attire of a working cattleman. "This isn't a costume," I said. "Not like that getup of yours."

"What's wrong with how I'm dressed?"

Pushed back on my head was a sweat-stained white Stetson made of Shantung straw. I touched it with one forefinger and pushed it back another half-inch. "No self-respecting cattleman wears black felt in the summer."

Then I told him what else was wrong with his outfit.

"Nobody else has said anything," he said defensively.

"Trust me, son," I told him, "they were laughing behind your back."

He considered that for a moment and then asked, "Why aren't you?"

I shrugged. I knew what it was like to be ridiculed by men like my father and my brothers and I knew how hard I'd had to work after returning home before our neighbors accepted me back into the community.

"So, what's your name, cowboy?"

"J. C. Beck." It wasn't the name I'd modeled under.

"So let me take your picture Mr. Beck," he said. "Show people what a real cowboy looks like."

"Cattleman," I corrected, dismissing him as I returned my attention to my now-cold meal.

The photographer returned to the booth behind me, grabbed his hat, and left the diner while I tried hard to forget the way I'd felt when he'd touched me. After I finished and sopped up the last of the white gravy with the butt-end of a biscuit, I realized he hadn't left but was outside, camera in hand, leaning against a Japanese-made pickup truck dwarfed by my white Ford F-350 parked next to it.

I slipped Steve Carson's card into my shirt pocket, left a fistful of crumpled singles on the counter for Edna, and pushed out of the diner. As soon as the door opened, the photographer lifted his camera and took my picture.

"You don't give up, do you?"

"I know what I want," he said, "and I want you."

Squinting against the bright sun, I stared at the

photographer. I wanted him, too, but not the same way he wanted me.

So, we talked.

Carson spent the night at a motel fifty miles up the road and drove to the ranch before sunup the next morning. I introduced him to my father and my brothers and told them what he wanted.

My father looked him over and I was glad Carson had been smart enough not to try to cowboy-up that morning, instead wearing jeans, blue T-shirt, running shoes, and a gimme cap.

"We ain't posin' for nothin'," my father told him, "and you'd best not get in our way when we're working."

"I won't," Carson assured my father, and he didn't. He spent the morning capturing images of the men in my family as we went about our daily chores.

That afternoon, after stuffing ourselves with my mother's beef fajitas and sweet tea, Carson assured me he could drive a stick. So, I saddled up my quarter horse and had him follow me in my F-350 out to where most of the herd was grazing.

Away from my family things changed.

After we stopped, Carson climbed into the bed of my truck, and I circled the truck on my horse. Even though digital technology had replaced film since I had last been on the business end of a camera lens, I still knew how to pose. Moving with the light, I presented my best side to Carson, tilted my head forward and back, turned it left and right, and did all that I could to ensure that he had the best possible shots.

Then I climbed off my horse and Carson climbed down from the truck. He took several more photos of me with my horse and with some of the Herefords, and some of me walking through the mesquite. When the wind kicked up for a brief spell, he even caught a few shots of tumbleweed blowing past me as I held onto my hat.

Working with natural light and without makeup artists, hair stylists, wardrobe people, and the herd of other necessary and unnecessary people I had learned to tolerate at high-end fashion shoots, we didn't stop until the sun had slipped low in the evening sky.

I hitched my horse to the driver's side door handle and sat with Carson on the lowered tailgate of my F-350, leaning close together to view the day's photos on his digital camera's small screen.

After examining several dozen photos, Carson put one hand on my jean-clad thigh, turned to me, and said, "The camera loves you."

It always had, but I didn't tell him that. Instead, I covered his hand with mine and slid it up my thigh so that he could feel my rapidly stiffening cock through the thick material of my Wrangler jeans.

Without a word, Carson set his camera aside. I tilted my hat back and pushed his gimme cap off, letting it fall to the dirt at his feet. I covered his mouth with mine, and our tongues met in a fiery dance of repressed desire.

My hands roamed over his still-clothed body, just as his traveled over mine. He was slender but firm, with strong arms, trim waist, tight butt, and a full package. He found my belt buckle and undid it, unfastened my jeans and reached inside my briefs to wrap his hand around my cock.

My eyes snapped open. No man had touched me there in years and I worried that I would be too eager, too quick to come, and I tried desperately to think of something—anything—that might delay that moment. Instead, I remembered men and moments from my past— the photographer's assistant, the sugar daddy who wanted to make me his, other models, in the bathroom of a New York City nightclub, in the makeup trailer in New Orleans, on the beach in the Grand Bahamas. That was all behind me, memories I had repressed and needed to repress again. So, I pushed those thoughts from my mind and instead concentrated on events happening right then, right there.

Soon I sat on the tailgate with my jeans and my briefs bunched around my boots, and Carson stood before me. I leaned back on the pickup's bed, bracing myself with my hands, my erect cock jutting up like a saddle horn from the graying thatch of my pubic hair.

When the photographer bent forward and took the swollen head of my cock in his mouth, I saw the last vestiges of the sun slip behind the horizon, and I moaned with pleasure. He licked away the glistening drop of pre-come, painted the head of my cock with his tongue, and then slowly took my entire length into his oral cavity.

Carson drew back until his teeth caught on my glans and then did it again. As his head bobbed up and down in my lap, the photographer reached between my thighs, palmed my nut sac, and teased the sensitive spot behind my sac with the tip of one finger.

My hips began rising to meet his descending face and then I wrapped my hands around the back of his head. I held him as my hips moved faster and faster and I knew couldn't restrain myself much longer.

When Carson squeezed my swollen sac, I came, firing a thick wad of hot spunk against the back of his throat. He swallowed and swallowed again.

He held me in his mouth until my cock softened and withdrew. Then Carson straightened up and stared into my eyes. He said, "I've wanted to do that ever since I saw you in the diner."

"I wish you hadn't waited so long," I told him. "I thought I was going to explode."

I wrapped one hand around the back of his head and pulled him forward. I kissed him again, a deep, penetrating kiss that had me tasting my own come, and I felt my cock begin to snake back to life.

The closest thing either of us had to lube was a half-used tube of moisturizing cream I kept in the glove box of the pickup. I told him to get it, and while he did, I stripped out of my boots, jeans, and briefs and threw them into the bed of the pickup.

When Carson returned, I made him do the same. Then I spun him around and bent him over the tailgate. I smeared moisturizing cream on my middle two fingers and slipped them down the crack of his ass to his tight little sphincter.

I massaged moisturizer into his ass crack until he relaxed and I could slip one slick finger into his shitter shutter. I used my free hand to dribble more moisturizer down the length of his crack and was soon able to slip a second finger into him.

"Quit teasing me, cowboy," Carson said hoarsely.

I withdrew my fingers, grabbed his hips, and pressed the head of my cock against the photographer's sphincter. He pushed back as I thrust forward, and then I was in him. I drew back and pushed forward, holding his hips so tight I left bruises that we didn't notice until later.

I slammed into him again and again and soon discovered that Carson was less familiar with a stick shift than he had let on. He'd stopped my F-350 on a barely perceptible down slope, had left the truck in neutral, and hadn't set the emergency brake. My repeated pounding rocked the truck, and it began to roll out from under Carson.

He grabbed the tailgate but couldn't stop the truck's forward momentum, and I couldn't stop fucking him even though I saw what was happening.

"Let go," I insisted as the weight of the rolling truck began to pull Carson out from under me. "Let go!"

As the photographer released his grip on my F-350, I slammed into him one last time and fired a second wad of hot spunk deep inside him.

We stood together, my spasming cock deep in his ass, and watched as my truck rolled about fifty feet, my quarter horse walking calming beside it. The rolling truck startled some inquisitive Herefords that had moseyed in our direction as if seeking a how-to primer in doing it people style.

Carson started laughing first and I soon joined him. After he pulled away from me and straightened up, I wrapped my arm around his shoulders we walked barefoot and bare-assed to where the truck had come to a halt.

During the following year, Carson and I developed a relationship that went beyond randy sex and run-away pickup trucks. As he continued traveling around the country photographing all manner of contemporary cowboys, we remained in touch via cell phone. When his schedule permitted, he stopped at the ranch and spent a day or a night or several days and nights with me. Only occasionally, because cattle don't take weekends off, I drove to Austin to stay with Carson in his apartment.

The book slowly came together, but except for that one evening sitting on the tailgate of my truck, I never saw any of Carson's photographs. He told me he'd selected several photos of me, including some with my father and brothers, but never told me how they'd been used. I never saw page proofs and didn't know until the book was published and a copy presented to me by my lover that my photograph graced the cover.

There I was astride my quarter horse, a herd of Herefords in the background, a faraway look in my eyes, looking every bit the buff, weather-hardened cattleman I had become and nothing at all like the young fashion model I had once been.

"You shouldn't have put me on the cover," I told him. He still didn't know that I had once been a professional model. When I saw the smile on Carson's face begin to fade, I added, "But thank you."

I thumbed through the book and checked the photo captions, which, thankfully, identified me by my real name—J. C. Beck—not as Jase Beck, the name I had used back when I was modeling. I hoped no one would put the two together.

Two weeks later, as we were about to sit down for dinner—my parents, my brothers and their families, and Carson—the phone rang. We all had cell phones and didn't often receive calls on the landline, so my father stepped into the foyer to answer the ringing phone.

A moment later he called to me and handed me the phone when I joined him in the foyer. As soon as I pressed the handset to my ear, I heard Delray, my former agent-for-a-day. He said, "You're a hard man to track down."

"I shouldn't be," I said. My parents have had the same number for decades. "Why did you call?"

"You don't know?" he said. "You're hot again. You won't believe how many calls I get for handsome men of a certain age and that cowboy book with you on the cover is the talk of the town. Everybody in New York wants *you*. I'm the only person who knows who you really are, and I have a dozen advertising agencies and three magazines already lined up."

"I'm not interested."

"Not interested?" Apparently, Delray had become successful despite losing his first client. "You know the kind of money I can get you?"

"I left all that a long time ago," I explained.

Carson stepped into the foyer, and I looked at him. I had finally taught the slender photographer how to dress when he visited the ranch, and he wore a denim shirt, Wrangler jeans, and ropers. His Shantung straw Stetson hung from the coat tree in the hall, next to mine.

I said into the phone, "I have everything I ever want right here."

I don't regret traveling the world as a model, nor do I regret the wild adventures I had as a young man, but fashion modeling is a young man's game I had no desire to return to the bright lights of the big city. I had traveled around the world just to realize that I could find everything I ever wanted within spitting distance of my front door—wide-open sky, hard physical labor, and a committed relationship.

My former agent continued talking long after I stopped listening. I dropped the handset into its cradle and stared deep into Carson's eyes.

"What was that all about?" he asked.

The phone began ringing again, but I ignored it.

I had a lot to tell Carson about my former life. But that could wait. I took his hand and walked into the dining room where we joined my family.

DOCKERS

The summer I met Billy Griffin I was working on the loading dock at my uncle's beverage distributorship. After I washed out of junior college during my first semester, I spent much of the following spring sitting in my room reading disintegrating paperbacks I picked up from the nickel bin at the Tattered Cover and sporadically applying for jobs I neither wanted nor was qualified to do. Finally, as a favor to my mother, her older brother hired me for the night shift, and I worked through the witching hour loading soft drinks, energy drinks, and flavored water onto the trucks that would later visit grocery stores throughout the city.

The loading dock was neither heated in winter nor cooled in summer and we adapted as best we could. The hard physical labor melted away the belly fat I'd carried throughout high school and into junior college, and a few months into the job I was no longer embarrassed to remove my T-shirt when triple-digit daytime temperatures cooled to nighttime temperatures in the mid- to high 90s. I was hard at it one Thursday night, my Metallica T-shirt hanging from my belt and sweat rolling down my torso as if I were a wet sponge being wrung out, when I realized Billy had his eye on me.

"See something you like?" I asked the next time I wheeled a pallet of soft drinks past where Billy stood with a clipboard in his hand.

A senior majoring in business at the university, Billy was interning at my uncle's distributorship that summer, and he had been studying the night shift all that week. He arrived each evening smelling of spicy aftershave, his square jaw freshly shaved, his closely cropped blond hair lacquered into unmoving perfection, wearing a form-fitting polo shirt over his broad chest, a pair of chinos with knife-sharp creases ironed into them, and highly polished burgundy tassel loafers. He left each morning seemingly unchanged, his appearance as fresh as when he'd arrived, and the men on the dock had taken to calling him a mannequin.

"Yeah," Billy replied, just loud enough for me to hear but not loud enough for the sound of his voice to reach any of the other guys, "your ass."

Without a snappy comeback, I kept moving, glad I was walking away from Billy because I felt my cheeks warm, and I worried the blush would spread to my neck and my shoulders and be visible from behind. I didn't know if Billy was serious or if he was teasing me, so I took extra time inside the delivery truck, positioning the pallet with more care than usual. Ever since I'd first seen him walking through the warehouse with my uncle, I'd had fantasies of giving myself to Billy, but I hadn't acted on them because I didn't know if he loaded front to back or back to front. I closed my eyes and for a moment let those fantasies wash over me. Then I glanced at the computer printout that had me loading the truck from last delivery to first, which ensured the driver would unload product at each stop along his route with a minimal amount of fuss and determined what I needed next.

The extra swagger I put in my walk when I exited the rear of the delivery truck was wasted effort. Billy was nowhere to be seen. Disappointed, I lost the swagger, and I finished my shift as I had begun it, humping pallets of pop into delivery trucks until the drivers arrived just before sunrise Friday morning. They compared their loads against their delivery routes and, once they signed off on our work, the night shift clocked out and headed home.

The parking lot emptied in a matter of minutes, the guys I worked with all headed home to whatever weekend plans awaited them. I had to rely on the chauffeur services offered by the city transit authority, and I walked three blocks from the distributorship to the nearest bus stop and stood staring in the direction of the rising sun, hoping the next bus would be along soon.

I wasn't paying attention to the early morning traffic, so I didn't notice the recent model Dodge Charger until it pulled to the curb and the passenger window slid down. From inside the car came a single word: "Hey."

I leaned over and looked in.

Billy Griffin sat behind the wheel. He said, "Want a ride?"

I opened the passenger door and climbed in beside

him. He had the car's air-conditioning on high and cool
air washed over me.

"I've had my eye on you all week," Billy said as he
eased the Charger into the anemic flow of traffic. "I like
the way your jeans fit."

I felt the same rush of heat I'd felt earlier that
morning when he'd commented on my ass, and my
reflection in the side mirror told me my face was pinking. I
said, "Thanks."

Billy reached across the center console and placed his
hand on my thigh. My balls tightened and so did my
sphincter. "I'd like to see you without the jeans," he said.
"Is there someplace we can go?"

"My house," I told him. I still lived with my mother,
but she worked dayshift at a nursing home on the other
side of town and would already be at work by the time we
arrived. I gave him directions.

Twenty minutes later Billy parked his Charger in the
driveway, and I led him through the house to my room.
Floor-to-ceiling bookcases covered two walls, and the
shelves overflowed with used paperbacks. I hadn't made
the bed before I'd left for work the previous night but
otherwise my room was clean and orderly.

Billy took everything in and then turned and jerked
his chin at me. "Lemme see."

I unbuckled my belt, unfastened my jeans, and peeled
them down to mid-thigh. My sweaty boxer briefs
followed. Billy wasn't interested in my rapidly swelling
cock, so he had me turn away and bend forward. I leaned

against one of the bookshelves, my hand only inches from a coverless Victor Banis novel I'd picked up a week earlier.

Firm from months working on the loading dock, my ass is smooth and nearly hairless, and Billy stepped close to cup my butt cheeks in his hands. He slipped one hand between my thighs and drew a finger along my perineum and up the length of my ass crack, pausing briefly to tease my sphincter. I tensed at his touch.

"You're tight," he said. "Are you nervous?"

My only previous experience had been with Del during Christmas break when he had returned home from college, and we'd gotten shit-faced on a bottle of bourbon he'd stolen from his father's liquor cabinet. There's a difference between doing it with a guy you've known for years and giving yourself to a guy you've lusted after but barely knew. "A little."

He stepped back. "Take your clothes off."

I did as Billy instructed and while I undressed, so did he. Billy obviously worked out, displaying gym muscles so unlike the muscles I'd developed loading trucks. His erect cock was long and thick and jutted upward in front of him. The thought of him sliding it deep inside me made me quiver with anticipation.

"Do you have lube?" he asked. "Because I'm not planning to dry dock."

I smiled at Billy's little joke and found the tube of lube I'd taken from my mother's nightstand that night with Del. Billy squeezed a dollop of lube onto his middle finger and then spun me around and bent me over my bed. His lube-slick finger quickly found my ass crack and slid down until his fingertip pressed against my tight sphincter. He stroked and teased, sending wave after wave of pleasure through me, until he finally slid his finger halfway into my ass hole.

Surprised, excited, and unable to control myself, I came, spewing come all over my unmade bed. And as I came, my sphincter contracted repeatedly, exciting me even more. Billy squeezed more lube into my ass crack and wedged another finger into me, opening me up even more.

Before long Billy removed his fingers and pressed the mushroom cap of his cock against my lube-slickened sphincter. Without any hesitation he drove it deep inside me, burying his full length into my ass. Del had not been as large as Billy nor as hard, and I bit my lip to keep from crying out.

He grabbed my hips and held me tight as he drew back and pushed forward, moving slowly at first and then harder and faster. Having him pound into me was more exciting than I had imagined those times the previous few weeks when I had squeezed my eyes tight against the daylight and had pleasured myself in my bed.

Billy's heavy ball sac swung against my perineum with each of his powerful thrusts, and the sound of man flesh slapping together filled the room until Billy couldn't hold back. He slammed into me one last time and held my hips so tight I couldn't have moved even if I had wanted to.

And he came.

Came hard.

Time didn't stand still but it might as well have. I don't know how long we stood like that, but Billy pulled away before I wanted him to. Then I sat on my bed and watched him dress. Before long he looked just as sharp as he had twelve hours earlier when he'd arrived at the loading dock.

He ran a finger along the spines of several paperbacks, spotted the Banis, and pulled it off the shelf. He fanned the pages with his thumb and read the barely attached back cover. Then he held it up. "Borrow this?"

I never let people borrow my books. The books never returned. But I wanted to see Billy again, wanted to feel his hands on my ass, wanted to open myself to him, wanted to feel his thick cock deep inside me, so I took a chance. "Yes."

We stared at each other for a moment, rich college boy and poor junior college dropout, and then Billy smiled. "I have to go."

"I know."

"We'll see each other again," he said as he held the book up. "When I return this."

I didn't believe him, but I said, "Okay."

I pulled on my jeans, walked Billy to the front door, and stood on the porch watching as he drove away.

Because beverage deliveries are made Monday through Friday, the nightshift works Sunday through Thursday preparing the trucks, and Friday was the beginning of my weekend. For that one week, Billy had worked the same schedule I did but he returned to the day shift the following Monday. I saw him only in passing each morning as he arrived at work and I walked to the bus stop at the end of my shift.

He finished his internship at my uncle's distributorship a few weeks later and then I didn't see him at all. I continued humping pallets through the hot August nights and cruising the stacks at the Tattered Cover no longer limited to the nickel bin. I'd found another Banis novel and was sitting at the bus stop reading it one morning at the end of August when Billy's Charger pulled to the curb and the passenger window slid down.

"Want a ride?"

My balls tightened and my sphincter spasmed as I remembered our coupling several weeks earlier. I closed the paperback and shoved it into my back pocket. As I approached Billy's car, I said, "I thought you'd forgotten me."

"I'll never forget that ass," he said. "I had things to do. They're done now."

The paperback he'd borrowed lay on the passenger seat. I moved it aside as I climbed into the Charger. When Billy eased the car away from the curb I knew exactly where we were going, exactly what we were going to do.

I just didn't know we'd still be doing it all these years later.

BATHHOUSE BACKSTABBER

I first met Joshua—Josh—at a cocktail party hosted by mutual friends. When I discovered we were the only two men attending without a partner, I realized we'd been set up, and I confronted Scott in the kitchen as he was pulling a tray of prosciutto-wrapped asparagus out of the oven.

"How could you?" I demanded. "I told you I'm not ready to date again, not after what Alex did to me."

Ever one to trot out a cliché when he thought it appropriate, Scott said, "It's been two months since you fell off that horse. Isn't it time to get back in the saddle?"

Alex and I had been together for nearly eighteen months when he dumped me for a grad student teaching in his department at the university. The sting of his rejection had hurt all the more because his parting shot had been to denigrate my writing as fit only for sub-literates who sounded out each word as they read, and I had not written a word since he dumped me.

As he moved the asparagus onto a serving tray, Scott said, "You know Alex was denied tenure last week."

"He was?" I hadn't heard, and the news brightened my outlook.

Scott handed me the tray. "Take these into the dining room and put them next to the seafood dip."

I did as requested, and then prepared myself a plate of appetizers from the dozens already crowding the dining room table. I had just made my last selection and was about to pop a cube of Swiss cheese into my mouth when I felt someone brush against my elbow. I turned and found myself facing Josh. He looked nothing like my ex. With closely cropped blond hair, sparkling blue eyes, and a square chin, he had the stunning good looks of a surfer.

"So, we meet again," he said with a smile.

"You realize we've been set up, don't you?"

"I figured it out a few minutes ago," he said. "Apparently you know more of these people than I do."

I admitted to knowing everyone else at the party, though some were only nodding acquaintances.

"I really only know Scott and Drew," Josh said. He put two stalks of the prosciutto-wrapped asparagus on his plate, added some Triscuits and a dollop of the seafood dip, and then we stepped away from the table to let other guests graze. "We met last week at a fundraiser for the symphony. When they discovered I was new in town, they invited me to this evening's get together."

"How new?"

"A month," he said. "I'm still getting my bearings. It would be nice to have somebody show me around."

Without thinking, I said, "Maybe I could do that."

"Maybe you could." Josh smiled. "So, what do you do?"

"I'm a writer." He didn't ask if I'd ever been published, so I didn't tell him that I hadn't. "You?"

"Photographer."

Scott interrupted our conversation. "How's the asparagus?"

"Looks good," Josh told him. He had yet to try it.

"And how are you two getting along?"

"Fine, thank you," Josh replied, "but you could have let us know this was a set-up. I might have dressed differently."

Scott winked at me, laughed politely, and moved on to a cluster of four men standing at the other end of the dining room discussing politics.

"What was the wink for?" Josh asked.

"Scott knows I wouldn't have come if I'd known he was setting me up."

"Oh?" Josh finally picked one stalk of asparagus from his plate, and I found myself unexpectedly watching his lips as he drew the head into his mouth and bit.

"It's only been two months since my last relationship ended."

Josh placed his hand on my upper arm, an impromptu act of commiseration that sent a warm tingle coursing through my entire body. "I'm so sorry."

Something about Josh's demeanor convinced me of his sincerity, which I hadn't felt from some of my long-term friends when I'd told them about the end of my relationship with Alex. Those who didn't mention that they'd seen it coming for months were too wrapped up in their own personal dramas to care one way or the other. Only Scott and Drew made any effort to console me, taking me to an expensive new restaurant where Drew, a tenured professor in the English department where Alex taught, repeatedly apologized for introducing us, and Scott insisted, as if he had inside knowledge, that "Karma's a bitch."

At that moment, with Josh's hand on my arm and his sparkling blue eyes searching mine, I melted a bit. Maybe, just maybe, I was ready for a new relationship.

I started writing again the morning following Scott and Drew's cocktail party. By Thursday evening, I had made good progress on a new short story and was writing the climactic scene where my private eye enters the bathhouse and confronts the killer, an English professor who had murdered his lover, a thinly veiled reference to Alex killing our relationship. I was interrupted when Josh phoned to ask if it was possible to tear me away from my keyboard for a few hours.

"What did you have in mind?"

"I have a photo shoot Saturday morning and was wondering if you'd like to join me," he said. "It'll mean getting up before dawn. I'm doing a 'day in the life' of the farmers market, so I need to be there when they start setting up."

"That's no problem."

I gave him my then-current address, confirmed what

time I needed to be ready, and was standing on the front porch of the English Tudor I was housesitting that semester, already fortified with three cups of black coffee, when he arrived Saturday morning in a recent model SUV.

I didn't have much to do but follow Josh around as he took hundreds of photos that morning, but we ate breakfast burritos and cream cheese kolaches prepared on the spot and we talked between shots.

As the morning progressed, Josh explained that he earned much of his living shooting photos for magazines, but he did other photography as well, including advertising and some wedding photography for close friends.

The farmers market was only open until noon, and just before the booths closed, Josh asked, "What about lunch?"

I looked around. "It'd be a shame to leave here without shopping," I said. "Why don't you let me fix lunch?"

I purchased organic vegetables, free-range chicken, bread fresh from a wood-fired oven, and half a dozen blackberry kolaches for dessert while Josh photographed the vendors packing their unsold goods and taking down their displays.

Instead of returning me to the house where I was staying, Josh took me to his loft, the third floor of an old warehouse converted into living space. Except for the enclosed bedroom and bathroom suite behind the kitchen area at one end, the entire loft was open and divided into separate functional areas through judicious placement of furniture and area rugs.

The end closest to the freight elevator was his work area, with two computers attached to large high-resolution screens, two desks, and a worktable. That led to the living area, followed by the dining area, and then the kitchen. Several large-format prints of Josh's photographs hung from the walls, and I admired them as we walked the length of his loft to the kitchen. All were of men in their natural surroundings, none of them studio portraits—a craggy-faced cowboy in a sweat-stained Stetson, a hirsute biker in his leathers, a shirtless construction worker with his yellow hardhat tilted back, a drag queen channeling Marilyn Monroe, and half a dozen more. None of the men captured in the photos were classically handsome, but all were appealing for their obvious self-confidence.

"These are prints from my All-American Male show last fall," Josh said. "My first gallery showing ever."

"That was here," I said, surprised. I named the gallery, and he nodded. "I was invited to the opening but had a conflict of interest." Alex had taken me to a lecture at the university, where I had listened to a snooty poet who couldn't earn a dime from her writing denigrate the crass commercialization of publishing. I hadn't enjoyed myself.

"It's one of the reasons I moved here," Josh explained. "There's a thriving arts community I hope to connect with."

By then we'd made it to the kitchen, a well-appointed work area gleaming with stainless steel appliances, and he showed me where he kept everything. While I chopped the vegetables, boned the chicken, added spices, and slid the result into the oven, Josh uploaded that morning's photographs from his camera to his computer. While lunch baked, I joined him in the work area, and we viewed his photos on one of the large computer screens.

As we went through them, he made notes about some of the photos, winnowing down the number he planned to present to his client. By the time we finished, he had selected three dozen and lunch was ready to serve.

Josh set the table, poured two glasses of wine, and soon we were settled into place. Over lunch, which he raved about after only the first bite, he asked me, "So, where have you published?"

There it was, the question I dreaded because I had to admit I'd never been published. "I have several dozen short stories making the rounds," I said, "and I'm working on my first novel."

"You should let me read some of your stories."

"You like mysteries?"

"I love mysteries, especially the old stuff—Raymond Chandler, Dashiell Hammett, all the Gold Medal books."

I brightened. Alex had always dismissed genre writing as pabulum for the masses, not worthy of his time or attention, and his attitude had done more to destroy my fragile creative spirit during our relationship than I wanted to admit. "Really?"

"Absolutely," Josh said. "My father got me hooked on the hardboiled stuff when I was a kid, and I've even taken jacket flap photos of a few mystery writers."

We talked about our favorite hardboiled novels before Josh brought the conversation back around to the inevitable follow-up question. "So, if you don't support yourself with writing, what do you do?"

I told him I was a housesitter, taking care of people's homes and sometimes their pets while they were away for extended periods of time. I'd become a favorite among university faculty during sabbaticals, long research trips, and teaching assignments abroad. "That's how I know Scott and Drew," I told him. "I sat their house several years ago while they spent the summer in Europe."

Though I didn't earn much, I didn't need much, and housesitting afforded me tremendous amounts of uninterrupted time at the keyboard to write. As soon as I could, I turned the conversation around and asked how Josh had made a career of photography.

"I learned from my grandfather. He had a studio in the small town where I grew up, and he was the go-to guy for portraits, wedding photography, and the like," Josh said. "I wasn't interested in studio work, so I took photos for my high school yearbook, worked as a stringer for my town's weekly paper, was photo editor for my college newspaper, and double-majored in art and journalism, both with a concentration in photography. After a few years working for a city magazine, I realized I'd rather be my own boss. I've been freelancing ever since."

We finished lunch, filled the dishwasher, and ate blackberry kolaches while Josh showed me his bedroom, where three of the four walls were covered floor-to-ceiling with bookcases filled with paperback mysteries he'd collected over the years.

Late afternoon we divided the leftovers from lunch

and Josh returned me to the English Tudor I was housesitting for a chemistry professor and her husband. He walked me to the door, told me how much he had enjoyed spending the day together, and made me promise to join him for dinner mid-week. I wondered if he would try to kiss me, but he didn't, and I watched from the living room window as he drove away.

As soon as his car was out of sight, I emailed five stories to Josh, including "Bathhouse Backstabber," the new short story I'd been working on when he invited me to accompany him on the farmers market photo shoot.

Over the years, I had shared my unpublished manuscripts with many friends and potential lovers who expressed interest in my writing, but those expressions of interest were often more polite than sincere, so Josh's failure to mention my stories Wednesday when we met for dinner didn't surprise me. After he still didn't mention them the following Saturday when we attended the symphony and had drinks with Scott and Drew, I suspected he never would. Though I was disappointed, Josh's silence was far superior to my ex-boyfriend's outright dismissal of my work, and by then I often caught myself daydreaming about Josh when I should have been writing.

We'd been dating for a month, seeing each other two or three times a week, when Josh took me to an expensive restaurant I had once mentioned in passing as one of my favorites. I thought we were going to celebrate his most recent assignment, a photo spread featuring lesbian motorcyclists with the working title "Dykes on Bikes," but I soon learned otherwise.

After our drinks had been served but before the appetizers arrived, Josh said, "I hope you don't mind, but I forwarded your stories to a friend of mine." He named a well-known mystery writer. "He's editing an anthology of new noir—crime fiction in the tradition of *Black Mask* but with modern settings. He wants to use one of your stories, if it's still available. He was going to mail this directly to you, but I convinced him to let me present it." He slid an envelope across the table.

When I opened the envelope, I found both a letter of acceptance and a contract for "Bathhouse Backstabber." I almost leapt across the table to smother Josh in kisses, but I restrained myself.

Barely.

Josh lifted his wine glass and made a toast. "May this be the first step in a long and successful writing career."

That night I invited him into my room at the house I was sitting that semester, and I spent several hours demonstrating just how grateful I was for what he had done.

Scott and Drew took me to lunch the next week after they learned of my first sale, and they congratulated me profusely. Scott trotted out yet another cliché, reminding me that success is only ten percent inspiration and ninety percent perspiration. Then he added, "And you've been sweating like a pig for years."

After we all laughed at Scott's comment, I explained how my inspiration for the story's villain had been my ex-boyfriend, and how I had ensured that Alex—named Alexis in the story—had died a slow, painful death when my private eye protagonist caught him in the bathhouse.

"It couldn't happen to more deserving person," Drew said. Then he told me Alex's contract with the university would not be extended when the school year ended, standard policy when tenure-track professors failed to make tenure.

Before I could react, Scott asked me about Josh. "I hear you two are like peas in a pod."

We spent the rest of lunch talking about Josh and how well our relationship was developing.

Almost a year passed before the anthology containing "Bathhouse Backstabber" was published, and by then *Ellery Queen's Mystery Magazine* had accepted a story, an anthology editor was holding another of my stories for further consideration, I had just finished writing my first novel, and Josh had asked me to move in with him.

Even though I had less than a month remaining on a one-semester housesitting assignment and no new assignments lined up, I had yet to give Josh a definitive answer. I was contemplating my response late one evening when my cell phone rang, and I answered it to find Alex on the other end of the call.

"I miss you," he said. I'd heard through the grapevine that he was teaching freshman composition at a community college across town, a serious step down from the upper-level British literature courses he had been teaching at the university, and he sounded as if he'd been drinking.

I couldn't resist being catty. "Did your grad student finally dump you?"

"He wasn't right for me," Alex said. "He never understood me the way you do."

"Well, you never understood me at all," I told him.

"Why don't you come over, and I'll make it up to you."

"I'm nobody's drunken booty call," I told him, wondering why I had been so distraught when Alex dumped me. But I was thankful he was providing me with the opportunity for much-needed closure. If I'd had more time to think, I might have come up with a great exit line, but I'd been spending too much time with Scott and resorted to a cliché. "You made your bed, Alex, now lie in it. Alone."

After I ended the call, I phoned Josh and told him I'd move in with him.

Several months after publication of the anthology containing "Bathhouse Backstabber," my story won a Robert L. Fish Memorial Award for best first mystery story by a previously unpublished author. Josh and I celebrated at the Mystery Writers of America awards banquet in New York, where Josh introduced me to the anthology editor who had accepted the story and where we met several of the writers who'd provided us with years of reading pleasure.

I thought my life couldn't get any better than the moment I walked on stage to accept my award, but I was wrong. Late that night, Josh led me onto the balcony of our hotel suite where we had a spectacular view of the Statue of Liberty. He dropped to one knee, opened a ring box, and asked me to marry him.

Of course, I said yes.

HOMECOMING

Keeping my two lives separate is tearing me apart. I'm a narcotics officer, and for several weeks or even for several months at a time I work undercover, unable to contact my life partner. When I do have the chance to return home, it is often without notice, surprising Joshua with my sudden appearance in our bedroom. He welcomes me each time, but I sense a growing distance between us, one that may become too great to overcome if the current investigation doesn't soon reach a conclusion, and I fear he will turn to another for the things I'm rarely there to provide.

We met when I was a rookie, just out of the academy and doing ride-alongs with an experienced officer. On my second day we were called to the scene of an assault—a mugging that had turned violent when Joshua refused to relinquish his wallet to a pair of street punks. He was sitting on the curb when we arrived, a bruise on his cheek already darkening, a young woman from a nearby salon sitting next to him. She had called in the assault while it was still in progress, but we had arrived too late to stop it.

Joshua gave us a lopsided grin and said, "They didn't get anything."

We did our job—taking statements, filling out paperwork, and so on—but I saw the way my training officer treated Joshua as if he were a suspect and not a victim, and I knew I would need to keep my sexual orientation a closely guarded secret if I hoped to advance within the department.

I don't know why, but I stopped at Joshua's apartment after I clocked out that night. My excuse was that he had refused medical attention at the scene, and I worried that he had made too hasty a decision. When he opened the door, I saw that the bruise on his cheek had darkened, but he appeared no worse for his encounter with the punks who'd tried to take his wallet.

I was out of uniform, so it took him a moment to realize who I was. When he did, he stiffened. "Yes, Officer Kirk?"

"Terry. Call me Terry," I said. "I wanted to assure myself that you were okay."

"Is this part of the department's new community outreach?"

"No," I said. I told him I was two days on the force and, until called the scene of his assault, had been involved with nothing more complicated than moving violations.

"Is that any reason to treat me the way you did?"

"No," I said. "My partner—"

"Don't blame your partner," he said. "You're responsible for your own actions."

He was correct, and I've carried that message with me throughout my career. "I apologize."

Joshua looked me up and down. "You want to come in? I'll fix us something to drink."

I hadn't thought that far ahead when I'd parked in front of his apartment building, but soon I sat on his couch, a Jack-and-Coke in my fist. Joshua sat on the other end of the couch.

Despite the bruise, he was an attractive young man, with finger-length blond hair, soft but symmetrical features, and sparkling blue eyes. He sipped his drink and eyed me over the top of his glass. After he swallowed, he said, "You didn't come here just out of the goodness of your heart."

I remained silent.

"You want me, don't you? I see it in your eyes. I saw it in your eyes this afternoon, but you were fighting your feelings then. Now...now you're not."

Joshua knew what I wanted without my asking. After setting his glass on the end table, he closed the distance between us. He placed one hand on my thigh and reached up with the other to brush the backs of his fingers along my jaw line.

I tensed, unsure what would happen next. My cock knew. It twitched and battled with the entangling folds of my boxer shorts as it began to swell and tent my pants. I downed the last of my Jack-and-Coke and set my glass aside.

"Kiss me," Joshua whispered, his face only inches from mine. "You know you want to."

I had not been with a man since before entering the academy, and I'd been careful while there not to reveal my carnal desires, but now I had no reason to hold back. I captured his head between my hands, careful of his bruise, and covered his lips with mine. We kissed hard, and deep, and long, our teeth clicking together and our tongues entwining.

As we kissed, our fingers fumbled with buttons and buckles and zippers and shoelaces, stripping away our clothes and strewing things around the living room. Soon enough we were naked, and Joshua knelt on the living room floor between my widespread legs as I sat on the couch. My cock stood at attention mere inches from Joshua's face and his warm breath tickled it each time he exhaled.

He wrapped one fist around the base of my stiff shaft and glanced up at me. Then he wrapped his lips around the spongy soft helmet head of my cock, hooking his teeth behind the glans, and painted my cock head with his tongue.

As he tongued my cock, Joshua began moving his fist up and down the length of my shaft, and each time his hand slid to the base of my cock, he took a little more into his mouth. When he had engulfed more than half of my cock, he drew back until only my cock head remained. Then he did it again and again.

A bit of pre-come escaped from the tip of my cock. He sucked it away. My cock grew harder, my balls tightened, and it was obvious to both of us that I was about to come when I began thrusting my hips upward to meet his descending mouth.

He grabbed my ball sac with his free hand and squeezed.

And then I came, firing hot spunk against the back of Joshua's throat. He swallowed every drop before he drew his face away.

He smiled, stood, and took my hand. "Let's take this to the bedroom."

His erect cock led the way. Once there he reached into the drawer of his nightstand and pulled out an unopened tube of lube. He opened the tube, squeezed a glob into his hand, and covered my limp cock with it. I began to regain my former stature, so I took the lube from Joshua and made him turn around.

As he bent over and leaned against the wall, I slathered lube into his ass crack, massaged it into his tight sphincter until it loosened enough I could slip a finger into him. Then I stepped behind him and replaced my finger with the head of my cock, pressing forward. His sphincter resisted at first, but there was so much lube slathered on my shaft and in his hole that it didn't take much effort to bury my cock inside him.

I drew back and pressed forward as he braced himself against the wall. My right hand was covered with lube, so I reached around and wrapped my fist around his erect cock. It was a little awkward to jerk him off while I was driving into him from behind, but I managed.

He came first, firing a thin stream of spunk against

the bedroom wall, and then I came, emptying my second load inside him.

We leaned against the wall for a moment while my throbbing cock slowly softened and finally slipped out of his ass. Then we collapsed across his bed.

We never did find the punks who had assaulted Joshua, but if it hadn't been for them, we might never have met, and our relationship never would have developed from that first meeting into something permanent.

For several years, until the department's attitude loosened up, we maintained separate residences. Then, less then a year before I was sent undercover, we purchased a house together—a house I visited far too infrequently.

Inside I'm still the rookie cop Joshua fell in love with; outside I'm anything but. I'd been clean-cut in those days. I'm not now, with greasy, shoulder-length hair, a scraggly beard, and tattoos I never would have gotten if I hadn't needed them to enhance my undercover persona. Each time I return home Joshua comments on the changes in my appearance, and each time I assure him that they are only temporary.

Three months has passed since I'd last been home. My hair has grown even longer, and I've gained a tattoo. I'm remembering our first time together as I push my way into our bedroom, led by an erection that quickly deflates when I see two shapes beneath the covers. Much as I'd feared, Joshua had taken another lover in my absence.

I switch on the overhead light, surprising both occupants of the bed. Joshua sits up, but his bed partner leaps at me, teeth bared, hackles raised, a growl erupting from his throat, and I back away.

Joshua calls the dog, wraps a fist in the black lab's collar, and assures me I'm safe from Rookie.

I laugh long and hard, collapsing on the bed with my life partner and his new companion. When I catch my breath, I tell him of my fear.

"You're right," Joshua explained, "I need company, but no man can replace you. Even so, I need someone I can love who will love me and make me feel safe while you're away. And Rookie does that."

I decided right then to request a transfer back to plainclothes and regular hours as soon as my current assignment ends. Then I scratch Rookie's head and gather Joshua in my arms.

My welcome-home kiss is everything I had hoped for.

GARDEN VARIETY

My fellow gardeners all tell stories about a "guy they used to work with" or a "friend of a guy they used to work with" who was seduced by the woman of the house where they were working. That's never actually happened to anyone I know, and no female client of our landscaping and lawn care service would interest me. It's not because some of them aren't beautiful; it's because I'm not out of the toolshed. I keep my sexuality to myself to avoid the compost I would have to put up with from my co-workers.

Of course, my attitude changed when I was assigned to the Winchester property. Old Man Winchester had a two-story Tudor at the butt-end of a cul-de-sac, a large place with simple lawn care needs. Because we were perpetually short-handed and I was accustomed to working alone, the Winchester property became my regular Thursday assignment. I mowed. I edged. I trimmed the hedges. And I tended a small rose garden near the pool house.

I worked through spring before I realized the young man living in the pool house wasn't the old man's grandson, and I worked halfway through the summer before I realized the exact nature of their relationship. By then Kyle was leaving his blinds open on Thursdays, and more than once while tending the rose garden I caught sight of him changing clothes or toweling himself dry after a mid-day shower.

At least ten years younger than me, Kyle had a figure sculpted by good diet, long hours in the gym, and just enough time in and around the pool to turn his firm, young body an all-over bronze and his finger-length hair nearly blond. The gene pool he'd sprang from was kind to him as well, endowing him with a long, thick cock and heavy balls that he kept neatly groomed but not completely hairless.

One Thursday afternoon, while I was watering the roses with a garden hose, Kyle walked out of the pool house with a towel wrapped around his waist. When he reached the diving board he dropped the towel, revealing that he'd worn nothing beneath it. He stepped onto the diving board, walked to the end, bounced several times, his thick cock slapping at his taut abdomen, and then jack-knifed into the pool, slicing into the water with nary a splash. He surfaced halfway down the length of the pool and the smooth strokes of an Australian crawl carried him to the far end.

Kyle rose from the shallow end, water streaming from his body, and he climbed the steps out of the pool. He tilted his head back and used both hands to push his hair away from his forehead. The movement of his arms caused his chest to expand and his abdomen muscles to tighten.

By then my cock had tented the front of my sage-colored work pants.

He returned to the diving board and retrieved his towel. As he straightened up, Kyle looked directly at me and asked, "Having trouble controlling your hose?"

"Excuse me?"

"You can keep watering the concrete, but it won't grow."

I glanced down at the garden hose, saw that I was watering the walk, and shifted position so the stream of water splashed into the rose garden.

Kyle toweled his hair and then draped the towel around his shoulders. "You spend a lot of time watching me."

I couldn't deny it, so I shrugged.

"You like what you see, Doug?" He knew my name because it was embroidered above my shirt pocket.

I tried to maintain eye contact, but I couldn't. I kept glancing down at Kyle's still-wet package. The water in the pool must have been warm because I saw no evidence of shrinkage. "I need to get back to work."

"You were almost finished," Kyle said. "The rose garden's the last thing you do."

He'd been paying as much attention to me the previous weeks as I'd been paying to him.

"Winchester's away," he continued. "He won't be back until evening."

I pulled a kerchief from my hip pocket. I used it to mop my brow and the back of my neck.

"I have cold beer inside."

I returned the kerchief to my pocket and glanced at my watch. I didn't have any other clients on Thursday, and I wasn't due back at the office for two hours. "Maybe one."

Kyle turned and walked inside. I turned off the water and followed him. The pool house hadn't been designed as a guesthouse but had been converted. Three louvered doors on one wall led to closet-sized changing rooms and a fourth door led to a bathroom with a shower; a built-in bar with a mini-fridge and a microwave occupied the second wall; a flat screen television filled the third; and the fourth wall was all glass, the blinds open to let late-afternoon sun stream into the room. A king-size bed occupied much of the main room, and it hadn't been made.

Kyle had opened two bottles of beer and he stood in front of the bed holding one in each hand. I took one from his outstretched hand and downed half the bottle in one long swallow. The beer cooled me but did nothing to dampen my desire for the naked man in front of me. My erect cock still strained against the inside of my work pants.

He said, "You still look hot."

Kyle set his beer aside and unbuttoned my sage-colored work shirt. When he finished, I shook it off my shoulders and let it slide down my arms to the floor. Then I peeled off my sweat-stained T-shirt and dropped it to the floor.

I don't have pretty muscles—I work for a living—and my tan is a farmer's tan. My face, my neck, and my arms from the ends of my short sleeves on down to my fingertips are leather brown while the rest of my body has the complexion of a grub worm—a hairy grub worm. Kyle didn't seem to mind. He unfastened my belt, unzipped my work pants, and pulled my pants and boxers to my knees. They fell the rest of the way to my ankles.

Then he sat on the edge of the bed and reached out for my thick cock. He wrapped one fist around my stiff shaft and pulled me forward, causing me to shuffle toward him. He took the head of my cock in his mouth, hooked his teeth behind the swollen glans, and licked away the glistening drop of pre-come.

He pistoned his fist up and down my cock shaft until I began to thrust my hips forward and pull back. Each time I did that, Kyle took more of my cock into his mouth. Before long he released his grip on my cock, grabbed my ass cheeks, and pulled my groin tight to his face.

My entire cock disappeared into Kyle's mouth, and I felt his hot breath tickle the wild tangle of black hair at my crotch. Then I pulled back and thrust forward repeatedly, fucking his face so hard my balls slapped his chin. I grabbed the back of Kyle's head, threaded my thick fingers through his still-damp hair, and drove into his mouth one last time before I came.

I stiffened as I fired thick wads of hot come against the back of Kyle's throat. He swallowed every drop and, when my cock finally stopped spasming and began to soften, he licked it clean. Then he pulled away, releasing his oral grip on my cock, and laid back on the bed.

My feet were tangled up in my pants, so I could barely move. I turned awkwardly and sat heavily on the bed next to Kyle. I untied my steel-toed work boots and let them thump to the floor before untangling my legs.

"You have no idea how good that felt." Kyle licked his lips. "I haven't had a real man in my mouth for months. Sucking that old man's dick is like chewing bad calamari. If he doesn't remember his pill, I can work that thing until I'm blue in the face and nothing'll happen."

I stretched out next to the younger man. Up close he smelled of chlorine. "Then why do you do it?"

"You think I can afford this lifestyle without Winchester? I've been to Aspen, New York, London. I drive his Ferrari. I eat lobster and steak. I always have walking-around money. I wear designer labels clothes. I don't wear a uniform with my name on it."

I ignored the unintended insult. "Why aren't you in the main house?"

"Old Man Winchester wants me to come when he calls but doesn't want me in his face all the time."

Kyle placed his hand on my knee and slid it up the inside of my thigh, ending the conversation. My cock responded to his touch, beginning to rise before Kyle's fingers reached my crotch. Then, through some quick digital manipulation, he returned my cock to its former stature.

He rolled over and reached into the nightstand, handed me a crumpled tube of lube, and then rolled face down on the bed. I squeezed a dollop of lube on my finger and slid my finger down his ass crack to his tight little sphincter. I massaged him until he relaxed, and I was able to slip one finger into him.

Kyle moaned with pleasure as I stroked my finger in and out, and soon I was able to ease a second finger into him. As soon as I was able to do that, I positioned myself behind Kyle, grabbed his hips and urged him onto his knees. Kyle had his face planted in a pillow and his ass pointed at the ceiling as I moved even closer.

I pressed my cock head against Kyle's well-lubed sphincter and grabbed his hips. With one forceful push, I sank my cock deep into him. Then I drew back until only my cock head remained inside him before I pushed forward again. As I pumped into his ass, Kyle grabbed his cock and began jerking off, his rhythm matching mine.

He came first, spewing come all over his rumpled bedspread. I wasn't anywhere near orgasm, and I held tight to his hips as I pounded into him, not realizing until later that I was leaving his hips bruised from the strength of my grip. I pounded into his ass again and again and when I couldn't hold back any longer, I came with a roar and filled his ass with hot spunk.

I held his ass tight against my crotch until my cock stopped spasming, and then I pulled out in one smooth motion. Kyle collapsed on the bed as I sat back on my heels and tried to catch my breath.

"You'd better go now," Kyle said, still face down in the pillow. "Old Man Winchester will be home soon."

I was late returning to the office and turning in my truck. The supervisor asked if I'd had any problems and if I needed help servicing the Winchester account. I had to assure him I hadn't encountered anything I couldn't handle by myself, and, to convince him of that, I refused to claim overtime for the day.

Kyle and I spent much of the next several Thursday afternoons in the pool house, drinking beer and fucking like rabbits. The yard suffered from my inattention, but not so much that the average person would notice.

Our window of opportunity was small because we had to ensure that I left the property before Winchester returned home and that I returned to the landscaping and lawn care company office early enough that I didn't provoke additional questions from my supervisor.

In early September, Kyle's mood began to change. There wasn't anything specific I could put my finger on; he just seemed more distant, requiring less foreplay and encouraging me to leave immediately after we finished fucking. He even stopped the pretense of offering me a beer while I was working in the rose garden. He just stood in the window and motioned me inside.

The last Thursday in September I followed the usual pattern—mow, edge, head for the rose garden—but this time the pool house blinds were closed.

I didn't bother watering the roses. Instead, I pushed my way into the darkened pool house, where I found Old Man Winchester sitting on the edge of the unmade bed. He wore a smartly tailored three-piece suit and had a checkbook open on his lap.

"How much, Mr. Fowler?" He had the deep, steely voice of a man accustomed to getting his way.

"Excuse me?"

"How much to walk away now and never see Kyle again?"

"Is that what he wants?" I asked.

"That's what I want."

"Do you always get what you want?"

"Always."

I stared at the old man.

"If I see you here next week, I'll call and cancel the lawn care contract. Your employers will want to know why. Do you want me to tell them?"

I didn't respond. I still hadn't come out of the toolshed.

Winchester wrote a check, tore it from the checkbook, and then slipped the checkbook and his pen into his inside jacket pocket. As he stood, he folded the check in half. He crossed the small room and slid the check into my shirt pocket.

"Kyle speaks highly of you. I think he's going to miss you." Then Winchester patted my chest and smiled the smile of an old and exceedingly dangerous shark. "Finish with the roses before you leave, Mr. Fowler. They're looking a little droopy."

After I finished with the roses, I returned the truck to the lawn care office and asked my supervisor to give me a different Thursday assignment.

I didn't look at the check until I was home that

evening. I pulled it from my shirt and flattened it on my kitchen table.

$10,000.00.

I'd never seen that much money before.

I'll probably never see that much again.

I shredded the check and ran the pieces down my garbage disposal. Then I drank myself to sleep and called in sick the next morning.

When my fellow gardeners tell their stories about a "guy they used to work with" or a "friend of a guy they used to work with" seduced by the woman of the house where they were working, I don't say a thing.

Who would believe me anyhow?

WEST TEXAS WINTER

Winters are tough in west Texas. Cold wind rages across the northern plains at speeds up to forty miles per hour, and there's little in any direction to impede its relentless assault on man and beast. Cold fronts can drive temperatures down sixty degrees in a matter of hours, and every five years or so the summer dust storms are punctuated by winter blizzards. Cody Jessup fastened the buttons on his fleece-lined suede jacket and settled his black felt Stetson atop his head before grabbing his overnight bag and stepping out of the wind-rattled singlewide mobile home where he'd lived for nigh on ten years.

During winter, he wore his boot-cut Wranglers a size larger than his summer pair in order to accommodate the bulk of his long johns, and at that moment he was glad he'd remembered his thick cotton undergarments because the wind hit him full force and drove its way through the tightly woven denim. He held on to his hat and stepped quickly down the concrete steps. As he walked from the mobile home to his white F-250, the ground crunched with each step, and he left a trail of boot-heel-shaped impressions where they broke through the frozen crust. The boots leaving a broken-earth trail behind him were more the color of Texas dirt than the color they'd had coming out of the box many years earlier, and they fit his feet as snug as his socks, having long ago molded to the shape of his feet.

A full beard protected much of his face, and ice began to form in his moustache as he exhaled damp air. By the time he wrestled open the door and stepped up into his truck, icicles clung to his facial hair. The F-250 resisted his first two efforts to start it, the engine finally catching on the third try. Cody exhaled, not realizing until that moment that he'd been holding his breath. He switched on the heat and shifted the truck into gear.

Five miles of private road led to four miles of county road and eight miles of Ranch-to-Market road before he reached a state highway, and the F-250's cab finally felt warm as Cody began driving the ninety-three highway miles to the town where he would meet Kendal Smith. He'd been waiting for this day for more than two months and wasn't about to let the weather dissuade him, a good thing given that the wind turned his F-250 into a bucking bronc, threatening to toss the truck off the road or into oncoming traffic, and he wrestled with it the entire ninety-three miles.

Kendal's matching white F-250—a coincidence neither cattleman had ever remarked upon—crowded a parking space at the far end of the diner's lot, and Cody crowded the space next to it with his F-250. Heat still radiated from Kendal's truck, so Cody knew the other man had not been waiting long. He found the older man sitting in a window booth inside, nursing a steaming cup of black coffee. Cody slipped into the opposite side of the booth and let his gaze drift over the man he had driven so far to see. He wore his black hair shorter than Cody's, and he had finger-combed it behind his ears when he'd removed his Stetson. Just like Cody, he had let his facial hair fill in as insulation against the cold, and it, like the hair on his head, was threaded with gray. A heavy crow had left its footprints at the corners of Kendal's eyes. They weren't the only wrinkles he'd acquired over the years, though they were the ones most visible during winter.

"Rough drive," Cody said as he unbuttoned his jacket. "You?"

"Same." Kendal had driven a similar distance from his ranch near the Oklahoma border.

The two men always met at the same diner, nearly always attended to by the same waitress, a thick-waisted grandmother in running shoes who kept her fire-and-brimstone upbringing to herself but who prayed mightily for the misguided souls who crossed her path daily, and she squeaked over to slip a cup of coffee in front of Cody.

Without bothering to glance at the menu, they ordered chicken-fried steak with mashed potatoes and white gravy, side of carrots for Cody and side of corn for Kendal. Only the season—sweet tea replacing coffee during the blistering days of summer—and the available selection of pie altered their dining experience each time they met.

"What'd'ya think of the weather?" Cody asked.

Kendal glanced out the plate-glass window. "Seen it worse."

Their meals arrived and they ate, sopping up every drop of white gravy with buttermilk biscuits. Then Cody ordered a slice of blackberry pie and Kendal ordered banana cream, the waitress refilled their coffee cups, and they wolfed down dessert just as they'd wolfed down the main course.

One hunger satisfied, they left a healthy tip for the waitress, bundled up and walked outside to their trucks. Cody followed Kendal to a motel on the edge of town, a place they had visited every other month since meeting at a cattle auction in 2011. Kendal had made the reservation, paid cash for the room and collected a single key attached to a yellow plastic fob near as big as his belt buckle.

Before long they had nosed their trucks into a pair of parking spaces in front of the ground-floor room and Kendal had the door open. Cody entered first and tossed his overnight bag on the room's only chair, a threadbare thing that had seen the ass end of too many overnight visitors. Kendal closed the door and threw his bag on the dresser next to an aging television they didn't plan to watch.

Cody pulled the drapes closed and turned to the other man. "Been too long."

"Not much longer'n usual."

They began peeling off layers of clothing.

"I miss you," Cody continued.

"Can't be helped."

Cody knew that, but he also knew their irregular connections via Skype, when each would pleasure himself while the other watched, were poor substitutes for the limited time they spent together pressing flesh against flesh.

"I'm all sweaty from the drive," Kendal said after he'd stripped off the last of his clothes and stood naked before Cody, his thick, flaccid cock and heavy ball sac dangling from a gray-speckled nest of black pubic hair. Even bowlegged from a lifetime astride quarter horses, Kendal stood half-a-head taller than the younger man. "I wouldn't mind some company."

Cody finished undressing, laid his long johns atop his other clothing and followed the older cattleman into the sea-foam-green tiled bathroom, a room that not been renovated or even redecorated since its construction in the early 1950s. His older lover reached into the shower, brought the hot water to life and turned to face Cody as slow-warming water pelted the inside of the tub.

"You're just teasing me now," Cody said.

Kendal smiled. "I really do need a shower," he said, "but mostly I just want to get you all wet and slippery."

Cody stepped forward into Kendal's embrace and reveled in the feeling of the other man's sinewy, work-toughened arms wrapping around him. Their lips met, despite the abundance of facial hair, and they kissed long, deep and hard. And as they kissed, Cody's cock lengthened and stiffened and prodded the older man's thigh.

The water pelting the inside of the tub had grown

quite hot by then, and steam clouded the tiny bathroom before Kendal finally drew back. He adjusted the water temperature and then stepped into the shower. Cody joined him and the two men fit as snugly as beef in a cattle chute.

The tiny bottle of shampoo provided by the motel held barely enough to lather their hair and beards, but the motel-size bar of soap Cody palmed allowed him to soap his shower partner from face to foot, and he lavished extra attention on Kendal's package as he lowered himself to his knees within the confines of the shower. He soaped the other man's heavy ball sac and then, with the soap bar still in his palm, wrapped his hand around Kendal's stiffening cock shaft. He pistoned his fist up and down the entire length until Kendal's cock was lathered with soap. Then he set the soap aside, rinsed away the lather and bent forward to take the swollen purplish head of Kendal's cock in his mouth.

Oh, how Cody had missed this during the weeks they'd been apart tending to their respective herds of Herefords. The life of a cattleman was often a solitary one and that the two of them had found each other often seemed to him an improbability only slightly less likely than that Texas would someday legalize their union.

As warm water pelted his back, Cody slowly took Kendal's entire length into his mouth, something he had never done with another man and which he had learned to do to please his lover. Once his moustache was mashed flat against the wet mass of Kendal's pubic hair, he drew back until only the older man's cock head remained in his mouth. Then he licked away the drop of pre-come that oozed from the tiny slit crowning Kendal's cock head.

He took in Kendal's entire length a second time and, just as his lips reached the root, Kendal wrapped his thick fingers in Cody's wet hair and held the back of his head. Then, slowly at first, he drew his hips back and thrust forward. Cody held Kendal's muscular thighs as the older cattleman face-fucked him, his hips moving faster and faster, his heavy ball sac bouncing against the thick cushion of Cody's winter beard.

When Kendal's ball sac began to tighten and his strokes became more aggressive, Cody knew his lover was nearing release. He slid one soapy hand upward, parted the older cattleman's firm ass cheeks and pressed the tip of his finger against Kendal's tight sphincter. As he pushed his finger into the older cattleman's ass, barely pushing it in as far as the first knuckle, Kendal made one final thrust and his cock erupted within Cody's mouth.

Cody swallowed quickly and then swallowed again as Kendal filled his mouth with come. He held his lover's cock in his mouth until it stopped spasming and began to deflate. Then he stood, took in a mouthful of water and spit it toward the drain.

When the warm water finally began to cool, the two lovers rinsed off the last of the soap and shampoo, and then stepped out of the shower and toweled themselves and each other dry. Cody followed Kendal to the king-size bed, stopping only long enough to retrieve a tube of lube from his overnight bag and place it on the nightstand while Kendal threw back the cover and top sheet.

They joined each other on the bed and lay face-to-face in the darkened room. Their fingers traced random designs in each other's chest hair, and when Kendal drew Cody close, they kissed. They were in no hurry now and their kisses lingered. A gust of wind rattled the window, reminding them of the world outside, and Kendal pulled Cody tighter in his embrace, one more thing they could never do through Skype.

Cody's cock reacted to the proximity of Kendal's body, slowly stiffening until it pressed against Kendal's thigh. Kendal's cock, not quite as quick to respond following their shower, also began to rise. When Cody felt Kendal's cock begin to stiffen, he rolled over and faced away from the older cattleman so that they could spork.

As Kendal's cock lengthened and nestled in the crack of Cody's ass, Cody reached out and retrieved the lube from the nightstand. He squeezed a glob of lube on his fingers. Then he lifted his leg, reached between his thighs and behind his ball sac, and coated his sphincter with the slick substance.

Kendal took the hint, shifted position and pressed the head of his cock against the tight pucker of Cody's ass hole. After only a brief application of pressure, Cody opened to the older man and accepted Kendal's entire length. Kendal drew back and pressed forward a second time, and then reached over Cody's hip and took Cody's erect cock in his fist. As he fucked Cody from behind, he stroked the younger man's cock in counter rhythm.

The first few times they had fucked after meeting at the cattle auction, their sex had been fast and hard and over too soon, as if they were competing in a sexual rodeo and a winning ride was measured in seconds. As they had grown comfortable with each other, as lust had been supplanted by unspoken love, their carnal encounters had grown more tender but no less explosive.

Kendal's fist began pumping faster, and soon he was stroking Cody's cock twice for every slow thrust of his cock into Cody's ass. Cody came without warning, firing a thick stream of come across the bed. He grabbed Kendal's wrist to stop the pistoning movement of the older cattleman's hand.

As Cody's cock throbbed in Kendal's fist, his sphincter muscles clenched and unclenched around Kendal's cock. Half a dozen thrusts later, Kendal came for the second time since they'd entered the motel room, and he emptied his balls into Cody's ass.

The two men lay together, Kendal's warm breath tickling Cody's neck until his cock finally softened and he pulled back enough to withdraw from Cody. Then they pulled the covers up and listened to the winter wind assault the motel until they fell asleep.

They spent that night, most of Saturday, and all of Saturday night in bed. When they talked, they talked cattle prices, feed supplies and how the drought had impacted their herds. What they didn't talk about was how much they missed each other when they were apart.

Sunday morning, they returned to the diner for brunch, consumed eggs over easy, thick strips of bacon and stacks of pancakes. They washed it all down with orange juice and mugs of black coffee and stared at each other across the table until they couldn't delay their departure any longer.

"Best be on our way," Kendal finally said.

"Yep," Cody conceded. He grabbed his black felt Stetson, settled it on his head and then slid out of the booth.

Kendal followed and they walked out into the cold, thankful that the wind had died down sometime during the night. When they reached their trucks, the two cattlemen stared into each other's eyes. Then Kendal thrust out his hand and Cody clasped it. They shook hands and slapped each other's backs, their last physical contact before returning home appearing to others as nothing more than two friends parting company.

Then they climbed into their F-250s, fired up the engines and headed their separate ways, the warmth of their time together seeping away the more distance separated them, and the west Texas winter resumed its relentless assault on man and beast.

THE LOOPHOLE

I'd seen a few demons in my time—usually after bouts of heavy drinking—but I had never had one appear in my office in the middle of the day.

This one materialized out of thin air, completely bypassing both the law firm's receptionist and my hardnosed secretary, and it took a moment for the smoke to dissipate before I could see him clearly. He wore a sharply tailored black suit over a white shirt and crimson tie, and he stood in polished black wingtips made of Italian leather. Coal-black hair combed straight back from his forehead hung to his shoulders, and he was clean-shaven, with a cleft chin and a square jaw. To call him handsome would be an understatement, but he wasn't without imperfection. His smooth, unblemished skin trended red rather than flesh tone and the pupils of his yellow-tinted eyes were more feline than human. His cologne was heavy on the brimstone, and it stung my eyes and caught in the back of my throat. I coughed before I spoke. "Do you have an appointment?"

He laughed—a deep, throaty laugh of genuine

mirth—before he spoke. "You people slay me. You make us an offer and are then surprised when we arrive to collect."

I stared at him across the top of my desk. "What offer?"

"Last night you said you would give anything for one night of memorable sex," he explained.

I'd been drinking with Jeremy. I might have said anything, and an oral contract such as the demon described would not be unimaginable given the dismal state of my sex life. "And you've come to provide it?"

"It would be my pleasure," he said. "More importantly, it would be yours."

"Will I need to light some candles, draw a pentagram, sacrifice a goat, anything like that?"

"The candles would be nice," the demon said. "Makes for a romantic atmosphere."

"So, what's the deal?"

He removed a tri-folded piece of parchment from the inside breast pocket of his jacket and smoothed it on the desk in front of me. The language was remarkably straightforward for a deal with one of the devil's minions: One night of memorable sex in exchange for my soul.

I pricked my finger in the expectation that the demon would later finger my prick and squeezed out a drop of blood. I signed my name to the contract.

As the demon retrieved the parchment, a duplicate appeared before me. He folded the original and returned it to his jacket pocket. I slid the duplicate into a folder to be filed later.

"Nine o'clock," he said. "Be ready."

Then he disappeared.

I spent the rest of the morning and much of the afternoon completing my due diligence on the Everson eviction case, and I felt certain that no harm would come to my client if I presented an ultimatum to opposing council during our meeting that afternoon.

We met in my firm's boardroom. On my side of the table with me sat two junior partners, three paralegals, and my secretary. On the other side of the table sat a young man fresh out of law school, employed by one of the storefront legal firms that do pro bono work for those unable to pay a successful attorney's hourly rate. His clients—an elderly couple who were the last remaining tenants of a building my client planned to demolish—were refusing to move, even after receiving a legal notice of eviction and my client's cessation of electric and water service to the building.

After we exchanged pleasantries, I presented the ultimatum. "Demolition begins Monday."

"My clients won't move."

"Doesn't matter."

The young attorney had exhausted every legal channel earlier in the week and the only card he had left to play was pity. "They've lived in that apartment for forty-three years."

"And?"

"They have no place to go."

"Not my concern."

"They'll be homeless."

"Many people are."

"What about their cats?"

"They'll be homeless, too."

The young attorney narrowed his eyes and glared across the table at me. "Have you no soul?"

I closed the folder before me and said with a smile, "Our work here is done."

Jeremy and I had once been lovers, but discovered we were better friends than sex partners. One of the reasons Jeremy and I are no longer lovers is because he let himself go, adding weight and losing hair in equal proportions, while I was in great shape despite creeping middle age. Regular workouts at the gym, a little nip-and-tuck for the eyes, and a regular application of Just for Men allows me to pass for several years younger than I am.

But we still had much to talk about. He'd made his money arranging adjustable-rate mortgages for people who could barely afford their house payments before their mortgages reset, and he'd made even more money selling short the stock he held in many of the banks that held those loans, and I liked his attitude of win at all costs.

We met for dinner and drinks at our favorite restaurant. Over filet mignons and shots of Jack I told him, "I made a deal with one of the devil's minions this morning."

"A minion? You didn't even get the senior partner?"

Jeremy asked. "You've chewed up and spit out so many opposing councils that even the devil should know not to send underlings to your office."

"My demon certainly looked successful," I explained, "but anybody can dress the part. He made a rookie mistake, so I'm guessing he's fresh off the hell-bound train."

I gave Jeremy the complete story, from the moment the demon appeared in my office to the moment he placed the contract on my desk.

"And you signed it?"

"Without hesitation," I said with a smile. "What do I have to lose?"

By nine o'clock that evening, I had showered, shaved, manscaped, and prepared myself for the evening ahead by slipping into blue boxers. I was sitting up in bed, enjoying the feel of freshly laundered red silk sheets against my skin, had a trio of candles burning on my dresser, romantic music on the CD player, a fresh tube of lube on the nightstand, and a copy of my favorite pictorial magazine spread across my lap. I was planning to use the lube one way or the other.

At seven minutes past nine, the demon arrived in my bedroom with the same flourish of smoke as before, and he wore the same clothes he'd worn earlier that day. Luckily, he'd replaced the brimstone cologne and, unless I was mistaken, was wearing Heaven—the demon's idea of a joke, perhaps.

I closed the magazine and placed it on the nightstand. "About time."

"I apologize," he said. "I was finalizing an agreement with a Republican senator."

Except for the wet bar, my bedroom is simply furnished—queen-size bed, pair of nightstands, single dresser, and a chair in the corner. The demon sat in the chair and removed his custom-made Italian wingtips, revealing not feet but polished cloven hooves. Then he stood and removed his jacket, tie, and shirt, placing them carefully over the back of the chair. His broad, hairless chest tapered down to six-pack abs and a trim waist, and I felt my cock twitch in anticipation.

I asked, "Care for a drink before we begin?"

"A Bloody Mary," the demon said as I flipped back the sheet and slipped out of bed. "Hold the tomato juice, hold the consommé, hold the vodka, hold the garnishes."

That left Tabasco sauce, horseradish, and cayenne pepper. I mixed the demon's drink and prepared Jack and Coke for myself. While I sipped from my tumbler, he knocked his truncated cocktail back in one swallow.

While I finished my drink, the demon removed his slacks and I realized three things: he was completely hairless from the neck down, he had a prehensile tail at least three feet long, and, as if to compensate, he had a flaccid penis barely an inch long. I almost laughed at the sight of it. I could not anticipate any way that little nub was going to provide me with a night of memorable sex.

But I was wrong. His little nub grew on me, clear evidence that the demon was a grower, not a shower. The demon stepped forward, hooked a hand around the back of my neck, and held my head as he covered my lips with his. He thrust his tongue into my mouth, and it felt thick and hot and forked.

He shoved his free hand between us and slid it under the waistband of my boxers. He wrapped his hand around my rapidly inflating cock and tugged at it until it reached its full potential. My erect cock isn't the largest I've ever grabbed, but it's much more than a handful, and the demon had his work cut out for him as he stroked up and down the length of my stiff shaft.

As he jerked me off, he kissed his way down my neck, down my chest, and, as he dropped to his knees, down my abdomen, leaving behind a hot trail of saliva. He peeled my boxers down my thighs, revealing my turgid cock, and let them drop to my ankles. He took the swollen head of my cock in his mouth and painted the purple head with the tips of his tongue. As he cupped my heavy ball sac in one hand, he wrapped his forked tongue around my cock shaft and ran it up and down the length. He took my entire length into his oral cavity and his breath felt hot against my neatly trimmed crotch before he drew his face back.

As the demon began face fucking me, I looked down and realized his tail was snaking back and forth between his hooves. I didn't have time to think much about that as his bifurcated tongue did things to my cock that I couldn't have imagined, and I began pumping my hips back and forth.

He still held my scrotum in one hand, and he

squeezed my balls together, kneading them and roughly tugging on my sac. I tried to restrain myself, but I couldn't. I grabbed the demon's head and felt the nubs of his horns hidden beneath his hair as I thrust into his mouth one last time. I emptied my balls against the back of his throat, and he swallowed every drop.

He didn't give me a chance to catch my breath. He released his oral grip on my cock while it was still spasming, and he stood. He grabbed my shoulders and spun me around, bent me forward, and pressed the thick head of his flaming red cock against my sphincter. I hadn't seen him reach for the lube, but he must have because his cock was slick, and he rammed it into me like a hot poker through butter.

His cock was longer and thicker than any I'd ever had before, and it seemed to grow within me. When he drew back and pressed forward it felt as if it was at least twelve inches long. He grabbed my hips, his fingers turning to talons that punctured my skin. I couldn't pull away from him even if I had wanted to for fear that he would shred my skin.

Then the demon's prehensile tail snaked down between his thighs and up between mine, coiling around my flaccid cock and quickly bringing it back to life. He fucked my ass like a demon possessed, slamming into me hard and fast and without end. His tail jerked me off as it stroked my cock with a steady rhythm.

I came first, firing come across my carpet, but he just kept fucking me harder and faster, drilling into me until my knees were so weak they couldn't support my weight.

The only thing that kept me upright was the demon's powerful grip on my hips and his enormous cock in my ass.

I wanted to cry out the demon's name, but he had never given it to me, and I had to content myself with expletives and repeated commands to fuck me harder and faster.

When the demon finally came, he came hot and hard, slamming his massive cock into me one last time before erupting within me and spewing come like a volcano spewing molten lava. He howled, and the sound curdled my blood and made the hair on the back of my neck stand at attention.

When he finished howling, the demon asked, "Do you smoke after sex?"

Three years earlier I'd given up cigars at the advice of my physician. "No."

"I do," he said. "Do you mind?"

"Go ahead. Light up."

When the demon released his grip on my hips and pulled away, I fell onto my bed, rolled onto my back, and looked up. Smoke rose from his entire body as if he'd been aflame and had just had the flame extinguished.

I felt hot enough to start smoking myself and wanted nothing more than a few minutes rest, but the demon wasn't finished with me. By the time dawn peeked through the bedroom curtains we had fucked so many times and so many different ways that I had lost count.

After the last time, after an orgasm that had me howling, the demon calmly dressed, adjusted the knot of his tie, and looked down at my spent body sprawled across the tattered red silk sheets.

"Was it memorable?"

I knew I would never forget it. Out of breath, I said, "Yes."

"Then I kept my part of the bargain?"

"Yes."

"Someday I will return to collect my part," the demon said.

Then he disappeared, leaving behind only memories and a thin haze of smoke.

I met Jeremy for a late breakfast and told him about my night with the demon. I even showed him the ten puncture marks on my hips where the demon's talons had gripped me. I knew no man would ever please me the way the demon had, but I accepted that because I knew I had gotten the best of our deal.

The devil should never have sent an inexperienced demon to negotiate with an experienced lawyer because the demon had failed to perform his due diligence. If he had, he would have known that the best attorneys—and I am the best—are born without souls.

I smiled.

Poor demon.

His senior partner was certain to be raking him over the coals.

PLAY

SPORTING WOOD

The competitors, suppliers, vendors, and some of the ticket holders arrived the day before LoggerFest began, and all the motel parking lots in town were filled with pickup trucks and SUVs. Even campgrounds and RV parks near the lakeside festival grounds were filled with out-of-towners who had come for the three-day event.

Competitors—who referred to themselves as loggers or as lumberjacks and lumberjills—and their entourages came from all over the United States, Canada, Australia, and New Zealand to participate in the lumberjack competition that was the centerpiece of the town's annual LoggerFest. The night the festival opened to the public, the local bars were packed wall-to-wall with men in plaid, the women who accompanied them, and a few men like me.

I was there with Bear Wilson, my long-time companion. When other young men were wrestling, tossing around a football, and practicing free throws, Bear Wilson was turning Pacific Northwest forests into kindling. I didn't meet Bear until we crossed paths at a community college in Oregon where he was a sophomore member of the school's forestry club, and I was a freshman journalism student on the prowl for some hardwood. I interviewed him for the school newspaper and, as part of the interview, he allowed me to help while he practiced the single buck.

Bear was a big guy even then, standing six-foot-two in his wool socks and almost another inch taller in his thick-soled, steel-toe work boots. He had muscular arms, broad shoulders, thick torso, and tree-trunk thighs, and it was obvious from the bulge in his jeans that he was a shower, not a grower. He wore his wavy brown hair nearly shoulder-length, sported a bushy beard, and the mass of hair covering his forearms when he rolled up the sleeves of his plaid wool shirt suggested nothing less than the follicle forest I later discovered covering his entire body.

Then, as now, Bear only participated in one-man events, but the single buck requires a seconder—sometimes called a "wedger" or an "oiler"—to prevent the saw teeth from sticking by wedging the competitor's cut and by lubricating the six-foot, three-inch cross-cut saw blade as it cuts through a log that may be as much as twenty-four inches in diameter. Often referred to as the "misery whip" because of the physical toll on competitors, the single buck requires that competitors use equal amounts of technique, stamina, and brute strength. The winner is the lumberjack who cleanly severs a complete cookie from the roundwood log in the least amount of time.

Late that afternoon of our meeting, Bear took me out

to the old barn on the edge of campus where the forestry club practiced for lumberjack competitions. His usual seconder—an axeman who participated in the underhand block chop and the standing block chop—showed me what I had to do. Then with a stopwatch he timed Bear sawing a cookie off the end of a nineteen-inch white pine log while I lubricated the saw and wedged the cut. When Bear finished—two seconds off his usual pace—I noticed that the crotch of his jeans had tightened.

After the axeman with the stopwatch said he had to get to work and left us alone in the old barn, I gestured towards Bear's crotch and asked, "What do you usually do about that?"

He stared at me, his eyes narrowing.

"Because if I were you, I would be lumberjacking off..." I smiled at my own joke, but Bear didn't. I continued as I wiped my hands on my jeans, trying to remove the lubricant I had gotten on them. "But since it's just us in here, maybe I could try pole climbing."

He looked around the barn as if to confirm that we were alone. "Are you saying what I think you're saying?"

I'd gotten a certain vibe from Bear when I'd interviewed him earlier in the day and, in the brief time it had taken him to saw a cookie off the end of the white pine log, he'd eyed me in a way that implied much more than an interest in how I did as his seconder. I hoped I wasn't mistaken when I boldly stepped close enough to put my hand on his crotch and feel his erection throb through the tight material of his jeans. When the young lumberjack didn't push my hand away, I unzipped his fly, reached inside his jeans, and pulled his erect cock out through the front of his white briefs.

Longer and with greater girth than any cock I had ever held, Bear's erection seemed to grow firmer as I wrapped one fist around it and stroked up and down. I dropped to my knees on the barn floor and took his spongy soft cock head between my lips. I teased the tiny slit with the tip of my tongue, lubricated the entire head with my saliva, and then slowly took his cock into my mouth until about half of it had disappeared into my oral cavity. I drew back until my teeth caught on his glans, and then I did it again, each time taking a bit more of his length into my mouth.

As I caressed his cock with my lips and tongue, Bear unfastened his belt, unsnapped his jeans, and pushed them down his tree-trunk thighs until gravity took over and drew them down to his ankles. I pulled my mouth away long enough to untangle Bear's cock from his briefs and send them down to join his jeans. No longer confined, his pubic forest sprang free, and I had to push the hair back with both hands to keep it from tickling my nose each time I drew the entire length of his cock into my oral cavity.

Bear's hips began to move back and forth, his cock slipping easily into and out of my mouth, and I knew he couldn't hold back much longer. Despite wiping my hands on my jeans, I still had some of the single buck lubricant on my fingers, and I could smell it as Bear face-fucked me. I moved my right hand and cupped his heavy nut sac in my palm for a moment before I pressed the tip of my lubricated middle finger against his tight sphincter. Then his ass hole opened to my pressure, allowing my finger to slip deep inside him.

That was all it took. Bear stiffened and fired a thick wad of hot spunk against the back of my throat. I swallowed and swallowed again, and I held his cock in my mouth until his hardwood turned soft. I wiped my mouth on my shirtsleeve and I rose to my feet.

"How did you know?" Bear asked as he pulled up and fastened his jeans.

"How could I not?"

"No one else knows, Randy." He glanced around as if he expected someone to overhear us. "No one in the club and no one else at school."

"So, you haven't come out of the forest…?"

When Bear didn't laugh at my little joke, I knew how serious he was about his closeted status.

"It'll be our secret," I assured him, and I kept it, not mentioning our post-single buck activities nor our subsequent conversation in the profile I wrote for the student newspaper.

I became Bear's seconder after that, the only non-competitor attending events as part of the forestry team. I don't know if his teammates were unaware of our relationship or if they turned a blind eye because Bear was the primary reason the team brought home trophies from every lumberjack competition they entered. My role hasn't changed in all the years we've been together, and I still have no desire to compete. I'm only there to help Bear—

and because I like the feel of his hardwood between my cheeks.

During the years since graduating from the community college, Bear has participated in numerous lumberjack competitions across the US, setting us back tens of thousands of dollars for equipment, travel, and entry fees. Prize winnings have never covered all the costs, but an entire room of our house is filled with trophies and ribbons and certificates of merit, so who am I to deny Bear the thing he enjoys most in life? Though single buck has always been his primary event, he often participated in underhand block chop, standing block chop, springboard chop, and axe throw, avoiding events that involve power tools, extreme heights, and the possibility of ending up wet should he lose.

Bear no longer sports the Grizzly Adams look—these days his beard is closely cropped and his silver-threaded hair rarely longer than finger length—but he still favors thick-soled, steel-toe work boots, jeans, and plaid wool shirts in cold weather. I tend to dress more fashionably—except when I accompany Bear to a lumberjacking competition—because my position at the city magazine where I'm employed as managing editor requires it.

While Bear never sought additional education after receiving his associate degree, I transferred to a university and earned a BA in journalism before taking a string of jobs with suburban weeklies and small-city dailies as I worked my way up the journalism food chain. Eventually, I landed at the city magazine, and for years one of my portfolio pieces was the profile I'd done of Bear for the community college's student newspaper. That piece, my journalism degree, and my constant appearance at lumberjack events, provided me with the bona fides to pick up freelance writing assignments for various media seeking articles about timber sports.

So, neither Bear nor I were unfamiliar to the other competitors as we high-fived, fist-bumped, and back-slapped our way through the biggest bar in town, a dive of immense proportion where the bartenders wouldn't recognize a mixed drink more complicated than a shot of whiskey dropped into a mug of beer. We chatted with the pole climbers and the birlers, the chainsaw wielders and the axemen, the double buckers and the single buckers. They were a motley crew of flannel-clad competitors. Some, like Bear, actually worked outdoors in jobs requiring physical strength. Other competitors worked in occupations like mine that kept them indoors, behind desks. Despite the increasing number of lumberjills entering the timber sports, it was primarily a testosterone-fueled environment where glorified desk jockeys attempted to prove their manliness against real lumberjacks and real lumberjacks tried to prove they were king of the forest.

Even though Bear and I have been exclusive for most of our relationship, there was a time in our early thirties when we were open to other experiences. We visited bathhouses and had a few flings, but even then, we kept our sexual identities and our carnal desires to ourselves at lumberjack events until one spring when a serious rain delayed a competition and drove everyone indoors. Bear and I found ourselves sharing a half-circle booth in a small-town dive with Nigel Bruce, a blond axeman from New Zealand. I sat between Bear and Nigel, and the three of us knocked back beer while we bitched about the lousy weather. Well into the third pitcher, Nigel placed his hand on my thigh and complained that he hadn't gotten laid since starting his cross-country tour of US lumberjacking events.

I glanced at Bear as Nigel's hand slid toward my crotch.

"I've been sporting wood for weeks and not a one of these lads"—He used his free hand to indicate the other competitors filling the bar.—"has a clue what a bloke like me really needs."

My cock responded when his hand reached my crotch and cupped my nut sac through the thick material of my jeans. Nigel wasn't quite as big as Bear, standing just over six feet tall, but he had the same muscular arms, broad shoulders, and thick chest. I said, "And just what does a bloke like you really need?"

A grin split Nigel's face in two. "A game lad like yourself, Randy."

Another glance at Bear brought a slight nod in return, and soon the three of us paid our bar tab and walked out of the dive carrying plastic to-go cups filled with the remains of our beer. I'm not a small man at five-foot-ten but walking through the rain between Bear and Nigel as we made our way from the bar to our motel room a block away, I felt like a sapling in a redwood forest.

Bear's dualie was parked outside our room, and he stopped to retrieve from the glove compartment the tube of lube we'd purchased on our way out of town the day before. Then he unlocked the door to our room and the three of us pushed inside. Like usual back then, the room had two queen-size beds. Though Bear and I only slept in one of them, we always messed up the other so as not to generate unwanted attention from motel maids. We had no desire to face some small-town sheriff enforcing outdated laws just because some chatty motel maid had gossiped about our sleeping arrangements.

The rain had soaked our clothing on the short walk from the bar and we were dripping all over the carpet. We peeled off our clothing and I hung everything as best I could over the shower curtain rod in the little bathroom. When I exited the bathroom, I found Bear and Nigel watching me from different beds.

Nigel, on the bed nearest the bathroom, wasn't nearly as hirsute as Bear, and he had a scar on his left shin that looked as if an axe blade had missed its intended target. Bear had his share of scars—many of them hidden beneath his follicle forest—and, like Nigel's scar, they only served to enhance his manliness. Nigel's flaccid, uncut cock peeked out from the nest of his blond pubic hair, not nearly as impressive as Bear's when flaccid.

When I sat on the bed next to Nigel and put my hand in his lap, his cock quickly responded. Proving he was more grower than shower, his cock rose impressively to attention. I made him lay back on the bed, and he scooted up until his head rested on one of the pillows. I knelt between his widespread thighs, cupped his scrotum in the palm of my hand, and kneaded his heavy nuts. With my other hand I drew back the loose foreskin, revealing the swollen purple head of his fat cock and the glistening drop of pre-come that adorned it.

I bent forward and took the head of his cock in my mouth, sucked away the drop of pre-come, and used my tongue to coat his entire cock head with saliva. I placed my hands on each side of Nigel's hips and lowered my face toward his crotch. Because he wasn't quite as well endowed as Bear, and because I had become quite accustomed to orally pleasing the larger man, I was able to take Nigel's entire length into my oral cavity with the first try. I drew back until only his cock head remained in my mouth, and then I did it again.

From the corner of my eye, I saw Bear squeeze lube into the palm of his hand and then take his erect cock in his fist. As Nigel face-fucked me, Bear covered his cock with lube. Then I heard him rise from the other bed, but I couldn't see what he was doing. A moment later I felt his lube-covered hand reach through my thighs and grab my erect cock. Nigel began bucking up and down beneath me, trying to shove his cock deeper down my throat than it could possibly go, and I knew he wouldn't last much longer. As Nigel continued feeding my face, Bear's firm grip and rapid pistoning action brought me to orgasm almost as quickly as I brought Nigel.

The New Zealander thrust his hips upward one last time just as I lowered my face into his crotch—smashing his pubic bone into my nose—and then he came, firing a thick wad of hot spunk against the back of my throat. As I swallowed, I came in Bear's fist, sending a stream of come all over the bedspread between Nigel's thighs. As Nigel's cock spasmed in my mouth and I kept swallowing, Bear released his grip on my cock and stepped to the end of the bed. He grabbed my hips and pulled me backward, forcing me to release my oral grip on Nigel's cock, and I could feel the fat head of Bear's cock pressed against my sphincter.

He had been quite generous with the application of lube so, when he thrust his hips forward and pulled my hips backward at the same time, his long, thick cock easily slid into my anal opening. As Bear drew back and slammed forward, burying his cock deep within me with each powerful thrust, Nigel slid upward in the bed until he was able to sit with his back against the headboard and watch us.

Bear's heavy nut sac slapped back and forth as he pounded into me, and I knew he was about to come when his sac tightened. With one last, powerful thrust, he drove his cock all the way in and filled my ass with hot spunk. He held my hips tight and stood with his spasming cock deep inside me until it finally softened and slipped free.

After Bear pulled away, I slipped off the bed, found the cup I'd carried from the bar, and drained half the beer as a come chaser.

By then Nigel's cock was rising again, and for the next few hours, as rain continued to pound the motel roof, the three of us engaged in a variety of erotic activities that led to several more orgasms between us. When Nigel finally decided it was time to return to his own room, he finished the dregs of his beer, pulled on still-damp clothes, and stood in the open doorway taking one last look at Bear and me sprawled across one of the beds. Before he left, Nigel said, "You blokes sure know how to have a good time."

The next day Bear was off his usual pace when he competed in the single buck, but he managed second place, losing by two-tenths of a second to a much younger competitor who looked as if he, too, had been up half the night and whose seconder looked more hung over than satiated.

Not long after that, Bear and I recommitted to an exclusive arrangement, and we've never again strayed—with or without the involvement of our partner. And even though we now reserve motel rooms with a single king- or queen-size bed because we no longer worry about mouthy maids, we still don't parade our sexuality at lumberjacking competitions.

Which meant it wasn't uncommon for one of the sports' female groupies to hit on Bear. That night was no different when we finally found an open table near the back of the dive bar and settled into two of the four chairs surrounding it. A large-breasted woman we had seen at other competitions—one we had seen hanging off the arm of more than one of the other competitors over the previous few years and who was now at least one drink past sober—grabbed one of the empty chairs at one table, slid it around so it was next to Bear, and dropped into it.

She leaned against him, pressed her breasts against his arm, and whispered something into his ear.

"I'm certain you could," he replied with a laugh as he pushed her away, "but I don't need my wood polished tonight."

She glanced across the table at me, and then told Bear. "You can even double buck me, if you want to."

That wasn't going to happen, not that night or any night, and Bear finally convinced her to leave after signing his name on her left breast with a Sharpie she produced from the back pocket of her painted-on jeans.

"There's something about you that's hard to resist," I told Bear after his newfound friend staggered away. I reached across the table and patted his hand before quickly drawing it back. "I know *I* can't."

The waitress stopped and took our order—beer for me, iced tea for Bear. Less than a year earlier he had stopped drinking and had changed his diet when younger competitors started besting him in competitions and his primary care physician suggested that beer and burgers were the primary cause of a thickening layer of blubber around his waist. He then began spending nearly as much time with cardio workouts as he spent with strength training, and the blubber melted away. Except for the gray threaded through his hair, the wrinkles around the corners of his eyes, and a slightly slower reaction time in the bedroom, Bear was in better shape than when we met as community college students.

We had come to LoggerFest after nine intense months away from the sport so that Bear could put his resculpted body to the test, and he had only entered the single buck competition. As we nursed our drinks, we looked around the room, picking out the single buckers and dissecting in rather snarky terms what we thought of their appearance. Two had put on weight since we'd last seen them, one had shaved his head to mask the expanding hair desert at the crown of his head, and another appeared to be trying to drown himself in beer. Two younger single buckers we knew only by reputation, having never competed against them, were markedly absent from the bar. One, we were told, was practicing tai chi in the parking lot of the motel where he was staying, and the other was a newlywed who hadn't been seen outside his motel room since checking in the night before.

"What do you think?" Bear asked.

"You'll smoke 'em," I said, not entirely certain. Age had slowed both of us down, but Bear had worked hard the previous months to counteract the effects of age and poor diet choices.

After finishing a second round of drinks and talking to several competitors who stopped by our table to ask why they hadn't seen us recently, Bear and I returned to our motel room. Our pre-competition ritual had changed considerably over the years, and I had him strip off his clothes and lay facedown on the bed. Then I lit scented candles, warmed the massage oil, and stripped down to my boxer briefs.

I straddled Bear, sitting on his ass so I could work on his upper body. Massaging a man as hirsute as Bear is a challenge, but I had years of experience. I poured warm oil into the palms of my hands and then started massaging his thick neck and broad shoulders, moving my hands outward from his neck and spine in straight lines because any circular motion would tangle his body hair. His tension slowly melted away and I could feel his muscles loosening the longer I worked on him.

I worked my way down his back, replenishing the oil in my palms as I went and sliding down so that I straddled his muscular thighs when I massaged his lower back and his buttocks. Soon I slipped off the end of the bed and stood as I massaged his thighs, his lower legs, and his feet. Then I made him roll onto his back and worked my way from his feet up his legs. By the time I reached the junction of his thighs, Bear had a massive erection that rose majestically from the forest of pubic hair.

Bear was completely relaxed, his eyelids at half-mast as I worked the insides of his thighs. I had not intended for the massage to turn sexual, but I couldn't help myself. I massaged his nut sac and his perineum, and then the full length of his erect cock. I covered it with massage oil as my hands slid up and down the stiff shaft. My strokes were slow and deliberate, and Bear's cock seemed to get harder the more I massaged it.

A drop of pre-come oozed from the tiny slit at the crown of his cock and I felt his erection begin to throb. I bent and took the head of his cock between my lips just as he came, and I swallowed and swallowed again as he fired a thick rope of hot spunk against the back of my throat.

I held Bear's cock in my mouth until it stopped spasming, and then I blew out the candle and curled up beside him in bed. He gathered me into his arms and, completely relaxed, fell asleep moments later. I didn't begrudge my lover for not attending to me because LoggerFest weekend wasn't about me; LoggerFest weekend was about Bear's attempt to return to the top of his game.

We slept well, awoke at first light the next morning, and prepared for the mid-afternoon single buck competition by eating a healthy breakfast and stretching. After long, hot showers, Bear and I dressed in black jeans and T-shirts provided by LoggerFest that were covered with festival sponsor logos. We pulled on light jackets to keep us warm until the competition started and then drove to the festival grounds.

The gates opened at nine, but competition wouldn't begin until one. When we arrived shortly after eleven, we found a growing crowd of people milling about watching various demonstrations, visiting vendor booths, and stuffing their faces with festival food of dubious provenance. After checking in, we watched a lumberjill use a chainsaw to turn logs into various forms of rustic sculpture that sold to festivalgoers for far more than they were worth. We returned to the competition area in time for the invocation and national anthem at one p.m. and watched the beginning of the open springboard chop and the intermediate underhand chop. With fifteen events packed into four hours, many of the competitions were concurrent, and we paid close attention to ensure that we were on hand for the start of the single buck.

By luck of the draw, Bear was in the last heat of the single buck, competing head-to-head against the young man we had not previously met because he was practicing tai chi rather than socializing the previous night. We watched as, two-at-a-time, ten lumberjacks each tried to cut a cookie off the end of a twenty-inch round white pine log. Dave Jewett set the world record for the twenty-inch round white pine in 2005 with a blistering speed of 11.29 seconds, but the world record did not appear to be in danger as two of the first ten competitors were disqualified and none of the others even broke the twelve-second mark.

When the judge called Bear's name, he unpacked his saw from its carrying case, we removed our jackets, and I pulled on my protective gloves. I checked the lubricant to ensure it was spraying properly and then stood on the log side of the saw opposite Bear, with the spray can in my right hand and the wedge in my left. The top of the white pine log was thirty-six inches from the ground, and Bear positioned himself with the length of the log to his right and what would become the cookie, once removed from the log, to his left. He secured his feet against the foot blocks, there to provide competitors with traction during the single buck event. Then he settled his saw in the small starting cut allowed by LoggerFest rules, and we waited as our opponent did the same.

Two timekeepers were assigned to each competitor and the official time would be the average of that recorded by the two timekeepers. The emcee began the countdown cadence and time began when he shouted, "Go!"

At that moment my entire world shrank to the pine log before me and the six-foot, two-inch saw biting through the wood in fast, even strokes. I sprayed lubricant on the saw blade and, when the blade bit deep enough into the wood, I placed the wedge above the blade, between the log and the cookie, careful to never touch the log, the cookie, or the saw with any part of my body.

Before another thought could pass through my brain, the cookie separated from the log and dropped to the ground.

And just like that, we were finished.

I looked at the timekeepers.

The announcer gave our competitor's time. "Eleven point nine nine seconds."

Our opponent had broken the twelve-second mark. I held my breath.

"And the winner, at eleven point nine eight seconds," said the announcer, "Bear Wilson!"

Bear grabbed me, hugged me, and then pushed me away. We had to wait until the awards ceremony that evening to collect Bear's trophy and $1,500 check, and then we would return to the motel to celebrate in private, using a different lubricant that would allow Bear to single buck me with fast, even strokes.

I was certain he would last far longer than twelve seconds.

BAREBACK RIDER

Every time the rodeo came to town, the local bars were crowded with hard-muscled men clad in tight-fitting Wranglers, snap-button shirts, low-heeled ropers, sweat-stained Stetsons, and belt buckles the size of dinner plates. Following the rodeo circuit were the wannabes and the used-to-bes, the groupies and the clingers-on, and they crowded into the bars along with the cowboys and the rodeo employees. Included in every crowd in every bar were the locals, the men and women who brushed against masculine greatness for one long weekend and lived on the adrenaline rush for the following twelve months.

Justin Longacre, a bareback rider who frequently finished in the money, rolled into town in his extended cab dually the day before the rodeo's first event, booked himself a room at the Motel 6 just down the road from the coliseum, and began to prowl the local bars. Justin had the sinewy build of a man who been stretched tight and held together by sheer determination. Unlike other bareback riders, the abuse he had endured seemed negligible: he'd smashed his face against the skull of a particularly spirited bronc, leaving his nose with a flat spot just above his nostrils, and a bad dismount had broken his left leg, giving him a barely perceptible limp.

In each of the bars Justin visited, men bought his drinks and women sidled up to him, offering themselves as if they were breeder cows. He always politely tasted the drinks and thanked the women for their attention before moving on, riding the local alcohol circuit the way he rode the southwest rodeo circuit.

In one bar near the Interstate, a well-lit place that catered to upscale out-of-towners, he had to explain to a buxom young coed what a bareback rider did.

"It's just me and the horse," he said. "No saddle, no stirrups, no reins, just a leather rigging that looks like a suitcase handle on a strap."

He explained to the attentive coed that cowboys grab the handle with one hand and throw their free hand in the air to keep from touching themselves or the horse during the ride. The cowboy must mark out when the horse leaves the chute, making sure that both spurs touch the bronc's shoulders. Then the cowboy spurs the horse from shoulder to rigging, doing his best to score points based on his strength, control, and spurring action during the eight-second ride.

"That sounds crazy," the coed said.

Justin had heard another rider describe it once and he'd repeated the description ever since. "It's the hardest eight-second ride on earth," Justin said, "like riding a jackhammer one-handed."

The coed lost interest when Justin failed to produce a

room key or a desire to pay her bar tab and she wandered away in search of a softer touch. Justin resumed his cruise through the central Texas town's ample supply of watering holes until he found himself straddling a red leatherette stool and leaning against the worn wood of a bar in a dark hole downtown, about as far away from rodeo people as he could get in distance and ideology.

"The rodeo must be back in town," said a soft-skinned young blond who settled onto the stool next to Justin.

"Yep."

"I thought I smelled cow flop."

Justin looked the young man over. Steven Pitt had the physique of an office worker, gym-toned but without the hard edges that only backbreaking outdoor work provided. He wore a dark suit, his rep tie still knotted at the collar. His close-cropped hair had been styled recently and his fingernails manicured. The faint aroma of expensive cologne settled around him.

"You a real cowboy, or a reject from the Village People?"

Justin stared into the younger man's eyes. "I'm a bareback rider."

Steven looked the cowboy up and down, as if searching for hidden meanings. "Why?"

"I like the risk," Justin explained. "Using a saddle just doesn't feel the same."

The young man considered for a moment, and then ordered two shots and beers. After the pug-faced bartender slid the drinks to them, Steven asked, "You in town long?"

"Just as long as the rodeo's here," Justin said. "Then I move on."

"Just like that?" asked the young blond. "No commitments?"

"I'm just looking for a good buck," Justin said. "I ride and I move on."

Steven lowered his voice and leaned into Justin. "You want to ride me?"

The question hung in the air unanswered until the two men finished their drinks. Justin followed Steven out of the bar and two blocks away to the bedroom of a third-floor walk-up apartment. Under Justin's watchful eye, Steven stripped off all his clothes except his tie, revealing a smooth, hairless body tanning-bed tanned the color of honey. Justin grunted his approval and peeled off his own clothes, revealing his own redneck tan. His face, neck, hands, and arms from mid-bicep down had the beef jerky color of a man who worked outdoors, while the rest of his hard body remained pasty white because it never saw sunlight. A dark patch of untamed hair at the juncture of his thighs provided a nest for his thick cock and heavy balls.

Steven dropped to his knees on the carpet in front of Justin and took the cowboy's rapidly stiffening cock into his mouth. As his tongue circled Justin's glans, he cupped Justin's heavy scrotum in his hands and massaged the cowboy's testicles. Then he used his middle finger to stroke the sensitive spot behind Justin's scrotum.

Justin reached down and held the back of Steven's head, feeling the stiffness of the young man's perfectly arranged hair as he pumped his hips against Steven's face. Soon he exploded in the younger man's mouth, and Steven swallowed every drop. After the young blond licked Justin clean, he stood, dug through his nightstand for lubricant, and then handed the tube to Justin.

"Ride me," Steven whispered as he turned around and bent over his bed. He placed his hands on the down comforter to brace himself. "Ride me hard."

Justin squeezed a drop of lubricant unto his finger and then applied it to Steven's rectum, teasing the younger man's fancy by pressing the tip of his middle finger against the tight sphincter, but not entering him.

After Justin withdrew his finger, he pressed the head of his cock against Steven's lubricated sphincter, pressing forward until he entered him. Then he grabbed Steven's tie, pulling Steven's head back as he drove forward, burying his cock deep inside Steven. Justin threw his free hand into the air as he drew back and pressed forward again. And again.

And Steven bucked, forcing himself backward to meet each of Justin's powerful thrusts. As Justin continued pounding into him from behind, Steven reached down and took his own turgid penis into his fist. He pumped furiously, coming across his comforter as the tie tightened around his neck and only moments before Justin came inside him.

Justin had ridden Steven long and hard and well beyond the eight seconds that would be required in the rodeo arena the next afternoon, and he continued holding the younger man's tie in one hand until his penis stopped throbbing. Then he dismounted, pulling his cock away with a barely audible pop.

Steven collapsed on the bed, clawing at the tie until he loosened it from his neck. As soon as he caught his breath, Steven rolled over to watch the cowboy.

Justin dressed, dropped a rodeo guest pass on Steven's chest, and said, "If you want to see how a real man rides, come tomorrow."

Justin let himself out, walked to his truck, and returned to the Motel 6. He eased his dually between two full-sized pick-ups outfitted with expensive tow packages, bought a diet Dr Pepper from a machine near the motel office, and returned to his room to drink it. Then he showered and climbed into bed alone because he always slept alone.

The next afternoon, Justin completed his first eight-second ride with a respectable score in the low eighties, and the pickup men swooped in to pull him from the still-bucking horse. After they lowered him to the ground, Justin looked into the stands. As soon as he saw Steven watching him, Justin knew he had a few more good rides ahead of him that weekend. In every town, no matter how big or how small, Justin Longacre always found a good ride. Sometimes it was a horse named Diablo, Crazy Eight, or Snake Eyes, and sometimes it was a man named Brogan, or Charles, or Thad. Justin didn't care which it was because he always rode bareback.

He lived to take risks. It was the cowboy way.

SLASH AND BURN

Slash rode goofy past the *No Skateboarding on Sidewalk* sign because he always rode on the sidewalk, and he looked in the store windows as he passed.

I rode through the shopping center parking lot, matching his speed but about five feet back. He darted among slow-moving shoppers still dressed in their church clothes and I dodged minivans and SUVs driven by soccer moms who paid more attention to the rug rats inside than the traffic outside their vehicles.

He wore baggy blue jean board shorts, a tight-fitting black wife-beater that revealed the tat sleeves inked from his shoulders to his wrists, and he had his finger-length black hair spiked. I wasn't nearly so brave, nor so fashionable. My blond hair hadn't been combed in days, and I wore jeans, a long-sleeved black hoodie, and thin black leather gloves. I was nowhere near as good as Slash, and I'd slammed so many times I think the palms of my hands will forever have the texture of coarse-grain sandpaper. That's why I'd started wearing the gloves.

As Slash approached the end of the shopping mall's

sidewalk, the old lady who owned the Sew-n-Sew at the south end of the mall stepped out of her store and yelled at him.

"Can't you read? How many times do I have to chase you hoodlums down? I'm going to call the police!"

She never did.

Slash smiled at her and did an acid drop off the curb at the end of the sidewalk. I kicked a little harder and caught up to him.

"Why do you torment her like that?" I yelled.

"Why does *she* torment *me*?" Slash yelled back. "Skateboarding's not a crime!"

We'd spent the morning at the skatepark with Tall Tony and some of the other guys and were on our way to my garage apartment, where I had an unopened box of frosted strawberry Pop-Tarts on the kitchen counter and two quarts of Mountain Dew in the refrigerator. It wasn't much, but it was more than Slash had offered me for dinner at his place two days earlier.

Slash and I had met at the skatepark, and we'd been together almost two years. I was taking accounting classes at the junior college, lived over my grandparents' garage, and relied on my parents for most of my pocket money, something they would only dole out if I maintained a B average. Slash, barely a year older than me, worked part-time at a bike shop and spent most of his available time at the skatepark perfecting his technique.

His uncle gave Slash his first skateboard, and as soon as he could nail some basic tricks Slash started entering contests. He wanted to turn pro, but he hadn't been able to attract the attention of sponsors. They didn't even comp him boards or other cool stuff. It wasn't about boarding ability, they told him, it's about attitude and marketability, and they didn't see anything in Slash that they didn't see in dozens of other boarders. Their attitude frustrated Slash because he didn't know how to make himself stand out from the pack.

I kept telling him that his time would come. Maybe that's why he hung with me even though I pretty much suck as a skateboarder. I might have been the only person in his life who believed in him.

We pounded up the stairs, parked our boards on the couch, and stepped into my kitchen, which was nothing more than the other half of my living room, with a counter, sink, fridge, and stove along the wall opposite the couch. Slash tore open the Pop-Tarts box while I retrieved the two bottles of Mountain Dew from the fridge. He handed me one of the foil-wrapped packs of Pop-Tarts and I handed him one of the two-liter bottles of Dew.

My apartment had only two rooms—the living room/kitchen and the bedroom—with a three-quarter bath accessible through the bedroom. I had decorated by taping posters of Tony Hawk and pictures of other boarders torn out of the skateboarding magazines to the living room walls. Some were pictures of famous skaters, and others were pictures of guys doing rad tricks. The bedroom contained a double bed and a desk where I did my homework, had more posters taped to the walls, and had a pile of dirty laundry in one corner because I was too lazy to carry everything downstairs for my grandmother to wash.

After we ate, Slash led me into the bedroom. He didn't have to say anything; I knew what he wanted. He wanted what he always wanted after a morning of boarding. He wanted me to go down on him.

When I unfastened Slash's belt, his oversized board shorts dropped off his slim hips and hit the floor, pooling around his ankles. He didn't wear anything beneath the shorts except the snake tattooed on his lower abdomen, and his thick cock already stood erect.

I still wore my gloves, and I wiped my palms on my pants to rid them of dirt from my frequent slams. Then I dropped to my knees, wrapped one gloved fist around Slash's turgid cock, and began pistoning my fist up and down. As I jerked off my skateboarding partner, I leaned forward and took the head of his cock in my mouth, hooked my teeth behind his glans, and painted his cock head with my saliva.

Then, while still pumping my leather-clad hand up and down Slash's fat phallus, I leaned forward, slowing taking in half his length before drawing back. His cock meat tasted salty and sweaty, and I licked the underside of his shaft as I moved forward and back. I did the same thing twice more before I reached around Slash, grabbed the firm cheeks of his ass, and pulled his crotch tight against my face, accepting his entire length into my oral cavity for the first time. Slash's heavy ball sac pressed against my chin and his dark, curly hair tickled my nose. I sucked and sucked hard.

My cock grew rigid in my jeans, but I couldn't do anything about it right then. I was concentrating on pleasing my skateboarding partner.

Slash's slim hips began to move as he drew his cock back. Then he pushed forward and drew back, his ass muscles tightening in my hands as he pushed forward. He grabbed the back of my head, wrapping his fingers in my hair, and fucked my face hard and fast, his heavy ball sac slapping against my chin with every thrust. Then Slash's cock exploded, and he shot wad after wad of hot come against the back of my throat.

I eagerly swallowed every drop of Slash's come before licking his cock clean. When I finished, Slash stepped backward. His flaccid cock dropped from my mouth and slapped against his thigh.

He stepped out of the blue jean board shorts pooled at his ankles and dropped backward on my bed. I admired his slim, muscular body for a moment, but something else demanded my attention. I had an erection, and it was tangled in my boxers. I reached into my pants to untangle my cock before standing. Then I stepped into the bathroom, dropped my pants, and settled onto the toilet seat. After I removed my gloves, I took my cock in my fist and quickly polished my knob.

Then I joined Slash on the bed, and we talked about nothing in particular.

Later, we headed back to the skatepark so that Slash could spend Sunday evening practicing, and we returned by backtracking along the same route that had taken us from the park to my garage apartment. I was half a block behind Slash as we approached the shopping mall because I had face-planted two blocks earlier, and I was trying hard to catch up. Many of the stores had already closed for the evening, leaving only the Dollar General open and the Sew-n-Sew turning out its lights as we approached.

Slash wallied the curb and continued onto the sidewalk. As he passed the front door of the Sew-n-Sew, several things seemed to happen at once.

A minivan with a soccer mom at the wheel and a prepubescent girl playing with a cell phone in the front passenger seat nosed into a parking space in front of the Sew-n-Sew, the minivan's headlights illuminating the front of the darkened store.

The old lady who owned the place, a bulky purse slung on one arm and heavy key ring in her free hand, stepped out of her shop and turned to lock the door.

A big guy in dark clothing ran around the end of the building, grabbed the old lady's purse, and ran away from me, going the same direction as Slash and gaining ground on him.

I yelled.

The old lady yelled.

The woman and the girl in the minivan yelled.

Slash glanced over his shoulder, saw what was happening, and did something I'd never seen him or any other skateboarder do. He stomped on his board's kickback as he dismounted, flipping his board into the air. He landed flatfoot on the sidewalk, grabbed his board out of the air with both hands and, holding it straight out in front of him with the deck perpendicular to the ground, spun almost 90 degrees and slammed the deck into the purse-snatcher's face, smashing the bigger man's nose and knocking him smooth out.

I reached the two of them at the same time the old lady did. She jerked her purse out of the unconscious man's hand and cursed him with that antiquated language she used when she yelled at Slash for skateboarding on the sidewalk.

"You going to call the police?" I asked.

"I'll call them," said the soccer mom, who had hurried to where we stood and already had her cell phone out. Her daughter walked behind her, holding her cell phone in front of her as if she was capturing everything with the video function.

I checked the purse-snatcher to ensure that he was breathing, but I didn't do anything about the blood pouring from his nose. I was more concerned with Slash's board, and he assured me that it was fine. Then three of us stood over the unconscious purse-snatcher while the girl started talking on her cell phone and Slash paced back and forth.

Two patrol cars arrived a few minutes later with lights flashing and sirens blaring. Two burly cops with more attitude than brains saw the bleeding scratches on my forehead from my face plant earlier that evening, and they rushed toward Slash before the old lady caught their attention and directed them toward the purse-snatcher, who was conscious but still laying flat on his back.

One cop called an ambulance and stood guard over the purse-snatcher while the other took statements from each of us. The old lady—Mrs. Winston—had the Sew-n-Sew's weekend receipts in her purse and was planning to drop them in her bank's night deposit on her way home, so she was grateful that her purse had not been successfully snatched. After the police left, she thanked Slash and then reopened the Sew-n-Sew so the soccer mom could purchase fabric to make something her daughter needed at school Monday morning. Slash and I sat on the curb until the soccer mom and her daughter finally left and Mrs. Winston was safely in her car and headed toward the bank.

Slash was amped up when we returned to my apartment. As soon as we had the door closed behind us and had dumped our boards on my couch, he pulled me into his arms and planted his lips on mine. Then he buried his tongue in my mouth.

His kiss was deep, hard, and aggressive. He practically tore my clothes off as we moved to the bedroom, and by the time we were naked we both had erections. I grabbed a tube of lube from my desk, squeezed a dollop onto my palm, and wrapped my hand around Slash's cock. I pumped up and down a couple of time to ensure that his shaft was completed covered. Then I wiped away the glistening drop of pre-come from the tip of his cock and covered his cock head with lube.

He spun me around and I climbed onto the bed, kneeling on the edge for a moment before dropping to all fours. Slash stepped between my legs, grabbed my hips, and pulled my ass toward him as he thrust his cock into my ass crack. The lube-slick head of his cock pressed against my sphincter and then, with one firm thrust, he buried his cock deep inside me.

Slash drew back and then plunged forward again, his strong fingers gripping my hips so tight I was afraid I might be left with bruises. He fucked me hard and fast, and when he came, he came hard. He slammed into me one last time and then held my ass tight against his groin while he filled me with his come.

Then he did something he didn't usually do. While still holding my hip with one hand, he reached around with the other and grabbed my turgid cock. I braced myself on one hand like a tripod and covered his fist with my free hand. I was so turned on by Slash's aggression and sudden interest in my satisfaction that I came quickly, spewing come over our hands.

When my cock stopped spasming, I pulled away from Slash and rolled onto my back. I still held his hand, so I pulled it to my mouth, wrapped my lips around his fingers, and licked them clean.

By the time I finished licking his fingers, Slash had another erection.

We fucked twice more that night before we finished off the Pop-Tarts and the Mountain Dew and fell asleep watching some really gay horror movie.

Slash went to the skatepark the next morning and I went to class at the junior college. I was sitting in the middle of the quad, a copy of one of the Norton Anthologies open in my lap and my skateboard on the bench next to me, when Tall Tony, a journalism major who boarded with us, did a wheelslide and came to a halt in front of me.

"Dude," he said as he stepped off his board, "did you see Slash's video on YouTube?"

I looked up. Tony stands well over six feet tall and he's thin as a rail. "What video?"

"The one where he jumps off his board and smashes a guy in the face," he said.

"When did you see that?"

"This morning. I was killing time before class when I saw it." He dropped onto on the bench next to me, opened his backpack, and pulled out his Apple laptop. "Let me show you."

Tony booted up his computer and logged onto the junior college's wireless network. He had bookmarked a video labeled "Skateboarder knocks out purse-snatcher" and a moment later I watched a replay of the previous evening.

I'd been right: the prepubescent girl in the minivan had been recording everything with her cell phone's camera, but someone had edited the video so that it started with the purse snatching and ended with the snatcher laying flat on his back. The girl had gotten excellent footage of Slash kicking his board up, catching it, and swinging it, so that I could see exactly what he did even though I knew I would never be able to duplicate the move.

"Did you see what he did?" Tony asked. "It was awesome."

"I know," I told him. "I was there."

He seemed surprised. "So, what really happened?"

I told him everything.

When I finished, Tony pulled an iPhone out of his camouflage shorts pocket, dialed, and pressed the phone to his ear. "Yo, Dad, you need to hear this."

Then he repeated everything I'd just told him about the previous evening and added, "I'll email you his cell phone number and the link to the video."

After Tony finished his call and email, he said, "My dad's a producer for *Channel 5 News*."

The next few days were wicked crazy. By the time I finished my last class of the day, a reporter from *Channel 5 News* had interviewed Slash down at the skatepark and Mrs. Winston at the Sew-n-Sew. That night I watched the story of the "Skateboard Hero" with Slash sitting next to me on my couch. The report included the girl's video of the event, Mrs. Winston being effusive about what a hero Slash turned out to be, and Slash telling the reporter that he hadn't done anything special. "I just did what anybody would do."

Within twenty-four hours the story of the Skateboard Hero was all over the network news, the cable news networks, and the Internet.

Slash finally stood out from the crowd. By the end of the week, he had a sponsor and had a new trick named after him: The Slash-n-Burn.

Slash's fifteen minutes of fame as the Skateboard

Hero didn't last long. The news cycle passed him by, but by then he was living his dream, earning a living as a pro skateboarder—first by demonstrating his move at various events and then by participating in and sometimes winning competitions.

I stayed in school, studied accounting, and helped Slash manage his money as his income grew. By the time I graduated from a four-year university, Slash had several endorsement deals—including a non-paying one for the Sew-n-Sew after Mrs. Winston made the mall's owners take down the *No Skateboarding on Sidewalk* sign—that I helped him negotiate, and we had moved into an old Victorian that I was renovating while he traveled.

I'd been right. I'd told Slash his time would come if he did the right thing.

He had.

And it had.

TOSSING THE CABER

A real man knows how to handle a big pole, and the caber toss at the annual Highland Games involves the biggest pole of any sport. The men who toss the caber are all big, burly men who make my knees weak and my pulse race when I see them lined up in their kilts and kilt hose, but they aren't the only competitors at the games.

In addition to the caber toss, the other Heavy Events—the stone put, the Scottish hammer throw, the weight throw, the weight over the bar, and the sheaf toss—all attract former high school and college track and field athletes who may not have been good enough to go pro but who remain eager to continue competing against other men. And they attract former athletes like me who no longer have any desire to compete, but who enjoy the companionship of athletes.

Scottish clans come from all over the region to compete in the Highland Games, and keeping everything organized requires dozens of volunteers. I work the competitors' tent, where Heavy Event competitors gather before and after events to adjust their kilts, tape their wrists, ankles, and knees, and guzzle Gatorade. I'm not there to play Peeping Tom, but I always enjoy seeing what Scotsmen—even pretend Scotsmen—wear under their kilts, and I have my chance in the competitors' tent, where I see everything from tightie whities to loose-fitting boxers to boxer-briefs to banana slings, all replaced or covered over by the chaste undergarment required of Highland athletes prior to each competition.

I try to keep my attention on the competitors' needs and not the rather explicit fantasies that run through my mind when I see big, burly men lift their kilts, but this past year one of my fantasies came true. I was cleaning up the competitors' tent late Saturday evening, long after the day's Heavy Events competitions had ended and most attendees had either returned to their campsites or were listening to the pipe and drum competition on the far side of the Highland Games site, when Derek Mackenzie, a caber tosser who favors tartan plaid boxers, pushed back the tent flap and stepped inside.

"I'm glad you're still here," he said as he crossed the tent to where I was working and held out his muscular left arm. He wore a black "Made in Scotland" T-shirt tight over his barrel chest, a Mackenzie muted green tartan kilt fastened around his thick waist and hanging to mid-knee, a black leather and silver sporran hanging at his groin, black kilt hose turned down at the knee over tree-trunk legs, and well-worn black ghillie brogues. His sandy hair flowed in wild curls to his shoulders and a full beard covered much of his face. "I need my wrist retaped."

"Been stroking the caber too vigorously?"

He smiled. "A caber as big as mine needs a lot of stroking."

I had him sit on the table while I used a small pair of scissors to cut the old tape away. His wrist was thick, his hands big and powerful, and I imagined them holding me.

To the back of my head, Derek asked, "What does a Scotsman wear under his kilt?"

It was an old joke, but I played along as I began retaping his wrist. "I don't know, what?"

"Your boyfriend's ChapStick."

He'd given it a new spin, and I looked up, into his pale blue eyes. "I don't have a boyfriend—" I started.

"Oh? Have I misjudged you?"

"—at the moment." I winked. Then I finished taping his wrist and patted the back of his hand. "There. Good as new. You'll be stroking the caber again in no time."

"I'd rather not do it alone," he said. "I prefer team sports."

His sporran had shifted to the side, and I could see his kilt beginning to tent at his groin.

"I'm a True Scotsman tonight," Derek said, informing me that he had removed the undergarment required of Highland athletes.

"And you're prepared to undergo a kilt inspection to verify that statement?"

"I am, indeed."

Derek was still sitting on the table, and I was standing between his widespread legs. I placed my hand on his knee and slid my fingers under the hem of his kilt. When he failed to stop me, I slid my hand along his muscular thigh all the way to his crotch, where I found his caber ready for competition. It might never win biggest in clan, but was of substantial length and ample girth, and I wrapped my hand around it. I slowly pumped my fist up and down, the heel of my hand against his pelvic bone and then upward until my thumb and forefinger reached the spongy soft mushroom cap of his cock head.

I wasn't satisfied just stroking his caber. I wanted more. I'd spent all day watching men in kilts and I was so turned on that I thought I might erupt in my jeans. As I dropped to my knees, Derek slid off the table and stood before me. I lifted his kilt and ducked my head under it as if I was about to take a picture with an old-fashioned camera.

His caber was as I had imagined it—long, thick, and rigid, with heavy stones hanging from the bag beneath, all surrounded by an unruly nest of sandy hair. I took it in my mouth, covered the cap with my saliva, and then slowly took his entire length into my oral cavity. I drew back and then did it again.

Derek pushed his sporran to the side so that it did not bang against the back of my head as I face-fucked him. Soon he held the back of my head through the thick material of his kilt and began thrusting his hips forward to meet each downward motion of my face. His heavy stones slapped against my chin.

Harder. Faster.

And then he came, erupting against the back of my throat, and I could barely swallow fast enough to keep his come from spilling from my mouth.

I remained under Derek's kilt until his caber stopped spasming in my mouth. Then I released my oral grip on it and slipped from under his kilt.

He took my hand and helped me to my feet.

"Did I pass inspection?" he asked.

I licked my lips. "You, sir, are a True Scotsman."

The tent flap opened and one of the Highland Games organizers poked his head in. "You should have closed by now."

"Derek needed his wrist rewrapped," I said.

Derek held up his hand to show off the fresh wrapping.

"We were just finishing up."

The organizer nodded and disappeared.

"We should continue this someplace more private," Derek said. "I have a bottle of Glenlivet in my cabin."

Single malt whisky and a cabin was enough to entice me, so I disposed of Derek's soiled wrist wrapping, cleaned the scissors with alcohol, and then switched off the light.

"How did you manage to reserve a cabin?" I asked as we crossed the grounds past the pipe and drum competition. There were only two-dozen cabins available, and most people opted to camp in tents, bring their motor homes, or stay in one of the motels scattered around the area.

"I put my name on the waiting list two years ago," Derek explained.

Before long we arrived at Derek's cabin. He reached into his sporran for the key, unlocked the door, and led me inside. The cabin was little more than a single room containing a queen-size bed, a dresser, and a nightstand. A window unit provided air conditioning in the summer; an electric heater provided warmth in the winter. A building thirty yards or so back the way we had come provided communal showers and restroom facilities.

After switching on the room's only light, Derek dug through his duffel bag and retrieved an unopened bottle of Glenlivet and two tumblers that had been wrapped in crew socks to prevent them from breaking. He didn't display any of the stereotypical stinginess of a Scotsman when he poured the Glenlivet, splashing a good three fingers of whisky into my tumbler and an equal amount into his.

He knocked his back and refilled his tumbler.

I sipped at the Glenlivet, not nearly the drinker my host appeared to be, using the whisky as much to rinse away the taste of Derek's come as to provide me with a slight buzz.

Half the bottle disappeared before Derek suggested I shed my jeans. I wore black hiking boots and I removed them first, dropping them with a pair of thumps to the wooden floor. Then I peeled off my socks, T-shirt, jeans, and boxers, and stood naked before Derek. I'd been a runner when I was younger, and I still had a runner's lean body, though the years since school had seen the addition of a few extra pounds and a loss of the muscle tone I'd once had.

Derek removed his sporran and set it on the nightstand. Then he pulled me close, covered my lips with his, and thrust his tongue into my mouth. He tasted of Glenlivet and something smoky, and his moustache tickled my upper lip as we kissed. He reached between us and cupped my rapidly rising cock in his hand, toyed with it for a moment, and then spun me around and bent me over his bed.

A half-used tube of lube appeared from out of Derek's duffel, and he squeezed a thick glob onto the two middle fingers of his right hand. He teased my sphincter for a moment, and then slid one slick finger into me. A moment later he slid a second finger into me, stretching me and preparing me for the caber that was about to come.

He flipped the front of his kilt over my back and pressed the spongy soft head of his caber against my sphincter. I was ready for him, and I pushed backward as he pressed forward, his entire length disappearing into me in one smooth motion.

Then Derek grabbed my waist and held me as he pumped into my ass, drawing back and thrusting forward harder and faster. By then my cock was swollen with desire, bobbing in front of me as Derek continued pounding into me from behind.

I wrapped my fist around my cock, realizing as I did that I wasn't nearly as long or as thick as Derek, but I certainly had no reason for shame. I began stroking myself and was surprised when Derek reached around and knocked my hand aside, replacing my fist with his own. He jerked me hard and fast, faster than he was slamming into my ass, and I came first, spraying myself in the chest because I was still bent over the bed.

And then Derek came with one last, powerful thrust that would have knocked me off my feet if my legs hadn't been trapped between Derek and the foot of the bed. He held me upright for a minute, maybe two, and then we both collapsed onto his bed.

We didn't talk much after that, but we did finish the Glenlivet, and we did fuck twice more before Derek fell asleep—or passed out—and I slipped out of his cabin. I showered in the communal facility before returning to my tent, and I slept soundly until one of the pipe and drum corps woke the entire camp with a rousing, screaming-cat rendition of "Reveille."

I stopped for hot coffee and scones at the volunteer tent, and then prepared the competitors' tent for the day.

I didn't see Derek until it was time for the caber tossing finals, and neither of us mentioned our night together. I re-taped his wrist and wished him luck, just as I wished luck to every one of the Heavy Event competitors I assisted in the tent.

One of the other volunteers manned the competitors' tent so I could watch the caber tossing finals, and I licked my lips with appreciation when I saw all the burly men in kilts waiting their turns. It took three men to carry the caber—a large wooden pole similar to a telephone pole—to each competitor, and then that competitor had to toss the caber into the air so that the top end landed closest to the thrower and the bottom end—the end that the thrower had been holding—landed pointing away from him. Scoring is based on how the caber lands as if viewed as the face of a clock. In a perfect throw, the caber lands at straight-up 12:00.

Despite my best wishes, Derek came in second, with a

toss landing only a few degrees shy of perfection. After the competition ended, Derek returned to the competitors' tent with me and had me remove the tape on his wrist.

"Are you going to be here next year?" he asked.

"I plan to," I told him.

"I've already reserved my cabin," he said. "I'll bring another bottle of Glenlivet and"—He glanced around to ensure that no one was listening to our conversation.—"and I'll let you toss my caber again."

My cock twitched in my jeans, and I smiled. "I'm looking forward to it."

A real man knows how to handle a big pole.

And I know how to handle Derek's.

SEVEN-INCH STRETCH

During the seventh-inning stretch, one of the cameras feeding images to the JumboTron always pans the skyboxes to show us poor bastards in the cheap seats what we're missing, and the last skybox is always dark, as if whoever owns it doesn't care for baseball. Danny and I sit in the cheapest of the cheap seats, in the bleachers behind right field where I've had season tickets for several years, and we never once thought we were missing anything by not partying with the rich people in the skyboxes. The beer and bratwurst crowd beat the sushi and champagne crowd every time, and surrounding us in the bleachers were fans that came for the love of the game and for no other reason.

At the beginning of every seventh-inning stretch, "Take Me Out to the Ball Game" blares through the stadium speakers and, just as the song begins, the JumboTron camera begins a slow pan of the skyboxes, always starting with the skyboxes above right field and ending with the skyboxes above left field. With nothing better to do during most seventh-inning stretches, I started timing the camera's slow pan. After a few games I realized the camera must be preprogrammed because the pan always lasted exactly ten minutes, and I started imagining what Danny and I might do if we could get into the last skybox during the seventh-inning stretch.

Danny and I met when we played ball for a junior college team, but we lacked the skill to turn pro or even to attract the attention of a four-year institution. After graduating from the junior college, we went our separate ways, coming together again in our early thirties when his employer transferred Danny to the city where I lived. Not long after that, we publicly resumed the relationship we'd kept hidden in college, and he moved in with me.

Our sex had been good the first time around, but it was better after we reunited because we were more experienced and more comfortable expressing our needs and desires. One of those desires—one in which no partner I'd had in the interim was willing to participate—was public sex.

The first time Danny and I fucked in public, we were standing on the balcony of our hotel room in Acapulco, enjoying Spring Break. Prior to that moment all our couplings had been in private, but we were both drunk, horny, and far away from anyone who knew us. I pulled my catcher's board shorts to his ankles, bent him over the balcony railing, and took him from behind while he shouted drunken nonsense to the people in the hotel pool four floors below. Somehow knowing that there were people watching us made me grow harder and last longer, and I felt the same rush I felt when I was on the mound in a ballpark filled with cheering baseball fans.

After reuniting, Danny and I engaged in public sex several times, but had never repeated a performance quite so public as our first experience in Acapulco. As the baseball season progressed, and as I paid an increasing amount of attention to the panning JumboTron camera and the empty skybox, an idea slowly developed, an idea that gave me an erection every time I thought about it.

I didn't tell Danny my plan until after I spent several innings during multiple home games exploring parts of the stadium I'd never previously visited. In addition to discovering a trio of specialty food vendors I'd not known about, I also found an express elevator that took passengers from the ground floor directly to the skybox level. I also learned that the same stairs that led to the upper decks also led further upward, and anyone could continue climbing until they reached the skybox level. I timed the walk from the right field bleachers to the stairs and then up to the skybox level, realizing I would be quite winded by the time I reached the top of the staircase unless I added more cardio to my twice-weekly workouts at the gym. On the other hand, descending a few flights of stairs did not seem to require significant physical exertion.

The first time I ascended the elevator to the skybox level an overweight security guard approached me because I lacked the appropriate paper wristband, and I was turned away when I conveniently couldn't locate my ticket. The guard, whose primary form of cardio must have been doughnut-lifting, stood with me until the elevator returned, but I remained long enough to see how the stadium waitstaff dressed—black shoes, black slacks, white chef coats with the team logo smartly embroidered on the left breast, and clear disposable food handling gloves—and to realize the staircases at either end were unguarded.

Two games later, the home team languishing at the bottom of the standings and in no danger of changing their position that evening, I climbed one of the staircases, learning that fans could enter and exit at every level except the skybox level. The staircases remained unguarded at the top floor because fans could exit the skyboxes and walk down the stairs but could not enter the skybox level from the staircases.

When I finally told Danny what I'd been doing when I slipped away during several home games, I saw the gleam in his eye that indicated the idea excited him as much as it did me. He was so excited that he gave me a blowjob in the backyard, in full view of people living on the upper floors of the three-story apartment building on the far side of the alley behind my house.

That weekend we finalized our plans after Danny revealed an unexpected connection to a stadium employee who, late Saturday evening in exchange for our solemn word that her identity would never be revealed, provided a skybox passkey and two white chef coats sporting the appropriate team logo. When we learned that a cold front would be blowing into town the following weekend, we spent much of Sunday afternoon and several evenings that week outlining our game plan and timing our sexual congress to ensure that we got off on time.

I shaved closely Saturday morning, man-grooming carefully so that my seven-inch Louisville Slugger would look its best when I stepped up to home plate. Danny and I wore non-descript clothing purchased specifically because none of it carried identifying logos, and we stripped off all jewelry before leaving home. We carried bulky jackets with the chef coats and three-hole black ski masks hidden in the lining, and we had clear disposable food handling gloves stuffed in our pants pockets. Danny carried a small tube of lube, and I carried the skybox passkey.

At the bottom of the sixth inning, our team so far behind that our only chance of winning was if food poisoning suddenly struck the opposing team, Danny and I slipped the chef coats from the linings of our jackets. Leaving our jackets on our seats, we made our way through the stadium and into the express elevator to the skyboxes. I jabbed the button with my elbow and the elevator doors closed. As the elevator rose, we slipped into the chef coats and pulled on the food handling gloves.

As soon as the elevator doors opened, the security guard took one look at us in the chef coats and turned his back on us. We looked like employees, so we didn't rate a second thought. We walked directly to the last skybox over left field and, after I glanced around to ensure that no one was paying attention to us, I slipped the key in the lock and opened the door. We hid the coats in a ceiling panel where our unnamed insider would retrieve them a few weeks later, after the commotion had died down, and by the time the seventh-inning stretch began and the loudspeakers blared "Take Me Out to the Ball Game," my cock was hard as a maple bat, we wore the ski masks, and we were in place by the skybox window.

When the first skybox appeared on the JumboTron screen, I dropped my pants and Danny dropped to his knees in front of me. He took the swollen mushroom cap of my cock in his mouth and painted it with his tongue. Then he grabbed my sac and kneaded my balls as he took the entire length of my seven-inch Louisville Slugger deep into his throat. The rough knit wool of the black ski mask tickled my denuded crotch as his mouth slowly slid up and down the length of my cock.

Someone in the seats below the skybox must have noticed what was happening above them because half-a-dozen fans turned to look up at us. Several dozen more fans quickly joined them.

I kept one eye on the JumboTron screen. When the slow pan reached the halfway point and the JumboTron camera pointed at the skybox high above home plate, I tapped the back of Danny's head. He released his oral grip on my cock, stood, spun around, and dropped his pants. Apparently, I wasn't the only one who primped for his big screen debut. Danny's ass cheeks were smooth as silk and sometime that week he had snuck away for an anal bleaching. He reached between his thighs, put a dollop of lube on the tight pucker of his ass, and then bent over in front of me.

My catcher and I had fucked in public many times, but we had never had an entire stadium full of people watching us. We were about to enter the big leagues. I took a deep breath, grabbed Danny's hips, and buried my thick, tumescent cock in his lube-slickened sphincter.

I drew back and plunged forward, maintaining a steady rhythm as I watched the JumboTron screen. By the time the camera caught us in the act, the fans in the stands below us were clapping in rhythm to my thrusts and I was about to explode. I pumped into Danny's ass several more times and then, when I knew I couldn't hold back any longer, I pulled my cock from his sphincter and spewed come all over Danny's ass cheeks.

A significant portion of the crowd applauded and cheered, but we didn't have time to take a bow. Even though all I wanted to do was catch my breath and let my heart rate slow, I knew it was time to go. As soon as the camera panned past us and we were off the JumboTron screen, Danny and I pulled up our pants and headed for the door, peeling off our ski masks just before we opened it. There wasn't time to hide the masks in the room, so we carried them with us as we stepped out of the skybox. The stairway door was directly across the hall, and we crossed at a brisk pace. By then the overweight security guard, who couldn't see the JumboTron screen from his station by the elevator and so had been told what had happened, was headed in our direction. He yelled for us to stop, as if we actually might.

We pounded down the stairs and separated at the next level. Danny exited the staircase and I continued down another level before exiting and easily melding into the crowd of fans returning to their seats at the end of the seventh-inning stretch. I abandoned the clear gloves in a trash can behind a hot dog vendor where they wouldn't be out of place, but the ski mask was harder to dispose of and it finally went into a dumpster in a side corridor not often used by the general public on their way to and from the food courts or the restrooms.

Danny was waiting in his seat by the time I returned to the right field bleachers, and I dropped into the seat beside him without comment. Quite a conversational buzz surrounded us as our fellow bleacher bums discussed the seventh-inning stretch entertainment. Knowing that they were all talking about Danny and me made my cock hard, and I had to lay my heavy jacket across my lap to hide the bulge.

I elbowed Danny and smiled. I had pitched and he had caught in a quite a few ballparks over the course of our high school and college career, but that night was the first time we ever played ball in a Major League Baseball stadium.

And we hit it out of the park.

MOON DOGGIE AND THE NIGHTSURFERS AT HAMMERHEAD BEACH

Hammerhead Beach, the site of the bitchinest waves in the northern hemisphere and home to a particularly ravenous population of sharks, had been off-limits to the general public for more than half a century. Most days the beach remained deserted until sunset, when the nightsurfers and the moonbathers arrived. Pale-skinned and cold-blooded, they didn't fear the sharks any more than the sharks feared them, and the two groups had co-existed peacefully for several decades.

Moon Doggie, the first nightsurfer to discover the once-remote beach, had come of age in the sixties, lusting after Frankie Avalon and not Annette Funicello, a time when few surfers dared come out of the Tiki Hut for fear of being shunned as a wooly woofter. Late one night at San Onofre, he and Butch Peterson—a middle-aged surfer who only visited the ocean at night—had wandered far from the bonfire where other surfers and their wahines were drinking beer and dancing barefoot to the music of Dick Dale. Moon Doggie had not returned to the bonfire that night and the next morning realized he'd developed an aversion to sunlight and a taste for blood.

He spent the next year with Peterson until the older nightsurfer's board smashed against a reef at Teahupoo on the southwest tip of Tahiti, breaking apart and sending a thick stake of balsa through his heart. Without Peterson's continued guidance, Moon Doggie learned to fend for himself in his new state of existence, forever twenty-three and still in search of the perfect wave.

The beach parties had changed just as Moon Doggie had changed. The nightsurfers and moonbathers built no bonfires for they needed neither the heat nor the light, and their only music was the sound of the waves racing to the shore.

Moon Doggie surveyed the moonbathers in their baggies and string bikinis as he carried his big gun across the sand and into the water. Like his, their skin was so pale it was nearly translucent, and because it reflected moonlight rather than absorbed it, they glowed with a faint luminescence.

After he strapped his leash to his ankle, Moon Doggie paddled out to where two other nightsurfers waited, but they didn't speak. Each remained attentive to the feel of the ocean waiting for the perfect wave to break, and Moon Doggie took his turn when it came.

After three hours of hot-dogging, Moon Doggie returned to the shore, lay down on his beach towel, and closed his eyes. He didn't sleep—that was reserved for daylight hours—but he did relax. For a time. Twenty minutes after he lay down, Moon Doggie's eyes snapped open and he rose on one elbow. The wind had shifted, and he smelled blood and testosterone.

He turned upwind and narrowed his eyes, trying to find the source. Around him, other nightsurfers and moonbathers did the same. He pulled on his huarache sandals, stood, and began walking north along the beach, following the scent. When one of the other nightsurfers rose and began to follow, Moon Doggie turned and glared, his gaze burning with an intensity that was no mere reflection of moonlight. The other nightsurfer, a recent convert still learning the hierarchy of the beach, hesitated and glanced around. When he saw that none of the others had risen to follow the scent, he returned to his blanket.

Satisfied that he remained the Big Kahuna and would not again be challenged, Moon Doggie walked alone along the sandy beach until it ended at a rocky outcropping fifty feet high that bisected the sand and jutted into the ocean. He climbed and, after he crested outcropping, looked down at a cove below where a pair of dick draggers—boogie boarders—were drinking wine from a box and fondling each other next to a roaring bonfire. They only had eyes for one another and could not see much beyond the circle of light cast by their fire even if they tried.

The two twenty-something dick draggers reclined upon a blanket, their board shorts already discarded and their boogie boards forgotten. Their bodies were taut but not overtly muscular, their skin bronzed, and their hair sun-bleached blond and blonder. Tyler lifted the wine box above Wayne's face and twisted the spigot handle until a thin stream of red wine trickled out. Wayne gulped down one mouthful and then another, but just as much wine stained his Vandyke and dribbled down to the blanket below his head as he swallowed. After several gulps, he pushed the box away and Tyler twisted the spigot closed.

Tyler tossed the wine box aside, leaned forward, and kissed Wayne. He sucked wine from the other man's facial hair before kissing his way down Wayne's neck, chest, and abdomen until he reached the closely cropped triangle of auburn hair nesting Wayne's ball sac and erect cock. He reached between Wayne's thighs and cupped his balls as he took the head of Wayne's cock between his lips. He licked away the glistening drop of pre-come that crowned it and slowly took the entire length of cock into his mouth. A moment later he drew back until his teeth caught on the other man's glans. Then he did it again.

The two boogie boarders had been flirting for several weeks, letting each other know of their mutual interest, but their evening visit to the beach had been Tyler's idea. He'd packed hot dogs, chips, wine, matches, and a new tube of lube. They'd brought their boogie boards—their pretext for visiting the beach though neither of them had intended to enter the water. Tyler had managed to light a driftwood bonfire, but they hadn't even opened the package of hot dogs. Instead, they had spent much of the time since their arrival drinking the wine and making out. Their board shorts had been discarded a scant few minutes before Moon Doggie crested the outcropping and stared down at them, and Tyler finally had Wayne exactly the way he'd dreamed about during all those weeks of flirting.

As he continued his oral manipulation of Wayne's cock, Tyler massaged Wayne's balls and stroked the sensitive spot behind them with the tip of his finger. When Wayne's cock began to stiffen, his hips began to move, and he reached down to thread his fingers in Tyler's hair, Tyler knew the other man couldn't restrain himself much longer.

Tyler sucked Wayne's cock deep into his mouth until the mushroom cap pressed against the back of his throat. At the same time, he pressed the tip of his finger against the tight pucker of Wayne's ass hole and pressed. As Wayne's ass opened to accept Tyler's finger, he came.

Though Tyler swallowed and swallowed again, he couldn't swallow fast enough and a potent mixture of his saliva and Wayne's come slid down the length of Wayne's shaft into his lap where it clung to his pubic hair.

Tyler slowly withdrew his finger but didn't release his oral hold on Wayne's cock until he had licked it clean.

The intoxicating mix of scents—blood, testosterone, come, wine, and burning driftwood—rose from the cove to tingle Moon Doggie's nostrils. He wet his cold lips with the tip of his tongue and felt the needle-sharp points of his canines as he watched the two young men on the beach below. He sported a woody and his erection strained against his baggies, demanding release. Torn between his desire to feed and his desire to fuck, Moon Doggie continued his silent vigil until the two dick draggers finally kicked sand over the embers of their fire and gathered their things.

By the time Moon Doggie returned to Hammerhead Beach, most of the other nightsurfers and moonbathers had gone. He grabbed his beach towel and big gun and carried them to his psychedelically painted Volkswagen panel van. After securing the surfboard to the roof rack, he drove several miles inland to the two-bedroom home he'd purchased several years earlier, and he closed the automatic garage door only moments before the first light of dawn found his neighborhood. He hurried through the house to the windowless basement where he would spend much of his day sleeping before going out that evening to feed.

Tyler crawled out of bed early that evening, showered and dressed for work at Tommy's Tiki Hut, a faux Polynesian bar where butt crumbs, waxboys, and gapers went to impress and hit on tourists staying at the nearby hotels. Unless employed by Tommy, few real surfers ever entered the Hut.

Before leaving home, Tyler sent Wayne a text about their evening together and was surprised when he hadn't received a response by the time he reached work. Midnight came and went, as did several of the female tourists and the faux surfers they invited back to their hotel rooms, before Tyler had a chance to look at his cell phone again. Wayne still hadn't responded so Tyler sent him another message, this one an explicit description of what he would do the next time they were together.

Tyler checked his phone again at the end of his shift and still hadn't received a reply from Wayne. Wayne didn't respond to the next dozen texts he sent and didn't return any of Tyler's phone calls. Three days after their carnal encounter on the beach, increasingly pissed that Wayne had used him and then put the slow fade on him, Tyler was ripe for Moon Doggie's mid-week midnight approach at Tommy's Tiki Hut.

The bar was quiet that night, with few tourists and none of the usual contingent of butt crumbs, waxboys, and gapers ready to hit on them, and Moon Doggie straddled a stool at the end of the bar nearest the exit. Though he still felt a little sluggish from his last feeding, he had another craving to satisfy.

Tommy's Tiki Hut specialized in umbrella drinks, but after taking Moon Doggie's order Tyler filled a mug with the cheap beer on tap and slid it across the bar to the nightsurfer.

Except for pale skin that made Moon Doggie look like a cavefish, he had the look of a surfer, so Tyler said, "I haven't seen you in here before."

"I saw you on the beach the other night with your friend," he said. "I wanted to meet you."

Tyler had only visited the beach at night once in the previous several months, so he knew exactly which night Moon Doggie meant. He said, "Wayne's no friend. I thought we had something, but that bitch used me and dumped me."

"That's a shame." Moon Doggie reached across the counter and took Tyler's hand in his. "You deserve better."

Tyler felt an unexpectedly cool tingle shoot through his body and his cock hardened. For the first time he looked into Moon Doggie's eyes and was mesmerized.

Moon Doggie said, in a seductive whisper, "I want you."

Tyler swallowed hard. "I get off at two."

"I'll be waiting."

Moon Doggie released his hold on Tyler's hand, breaking the spell, and slipped off the stool. He tossed a crumpled five-dollar bill on the bar, but it wasn't until a few minutes after the door closed behind him that Tyler realized the nightsurfer hadn't touched the beer.

The last two hours of Tyler's shift crawled past, and he rushed through the back door as soon as he clocked out. Moon Doggie waited there, leaning against his van, and through the open door Tyler saw the mattress covering the Volkswagen's floor. Any other time he would have thought twice about climbing into the van of someone he had met only hours earlier, but something about Moon Doggie made him difficult to resist.

Moon Doggie climbed in after Tyler, closed the door, and sat cross-legged on the mattress facing his nervous guest. Black curtains covered the rear windows, and another separated the front seats from the rest of the van, effectively cocooning them in darkness. Moon Doggie had inherited the van from Peterson and the curtains were only a small part of what Peterson had done to make the rear area completely light safe. They had spent many months sleeping in the van prior to Peterson's fatal encounter with a splintered surfboard, and Moon Doggie had spent several more until he purchased his house with its windowless basement.

Though Moon Doggie could see in the darkness, he knew Tyler could not. To provide light for his guest, he lit a string of tiny white LED Christmas tree lights strung around the inside of the van, and then he turned and stared into the nervous boogie boarder's eyes. He touched his middle finger just below Tyler's ear and traced the jaw line to his chin, lifting Tyler's face ever so slightly as he did. Then he pressed his lips against the young man's, feeling the warmth of Tyler's breath on his cheek as the boogie boarder relaxed and slowly exhaled.

Tyler's lips parted as Moon Doggie's kiss grew more insistent, and the nightsurfer thrust his tongue into the young man's mouth, feeling the heat of Tyler's oral cavity envelope it. The kiss was deep and hard and unintentionally stole the younger man's breath until Tyler pulled away.

As Tyler struggled to breathe, Moon Doggie unbuttoned the blue Hawaiian shirt Tyler wore for work, pushed it open, and rested his palm flat against the boogie boarder's chest to feel the young heart beating beneath the ribs. A moment later he pushed the shirt from Tyler's shoulders and let it slide down the young man's sun-bronzed arms. Then the tip of his tongue followed the path his finger had earlier, down Tyler's jaw line from his ear to his chin. Instead of traveling upward to the young man's lips, though, he continued drawing a wet line down

Tyler's neck. He let the tip of his tongue linger on Tyler's jugular vein, feeling the hot blood pulse beneath the skin. Had he not still been satiated by his most recent feeding, Moon Doggie would have been tempted to sink his teeth into the boogie boarder's vein and slowly draw out the young man's life force.

He resisted the temptation and drew his tongue down Tyler's hairless chest until he could suck one erect nipple between his teeth. He gently nipped it, not hard enough to draw blood but hard enough for the pain to cause Tyler to pull away. As he did, Moon Doggie pushed Tyler back on the mattress, grabbed his loose-fitting cargo shorts and boxers and jerked them down the younger man's legs to his knees, exposing his erect cock. When Tyler lifted his legs, Moon Doggie removed the young man's huarache sandals, pants, and boxers and tossed them toward the rear of the van.

Unlike Wayne, Tyler was a natural blond, not a sun-bleached blond with contrary evidence concealed beneath his shorts, and his cock rose firm and erect from the tangled nest at the juncture of his thighs. Moon Doggie wrapped one fist around Tyler's erection, thumbed the mushroom cap several times, and then released his grip. He stuck the ball of his thumb in his mouth and tasted the glistening bit of pre-come that he'd wiped from the tip of Tyler's cock head.

Then he dove forward, almost ravenous in his desire, and took the entire length of Tyler's cock into his mouth, surprising the young man. Blond pubic hair tickled his nose until he drew back and caught the back of his teeth on the boogie boarder's swollen glans.

The young man's hips began to buck up and down as he thrust his hips upward to meet Moon Doggie's face each time it descended into his lap. The nightsurfer could feel the increasing tension in the young man's hips and the way his cock strained against his lips, and he was prepared when Tyler finally erupted inside his mouth.

Just as the young man came, Moon Doggie pricked his dorsal artery with the tip of one tooth and drew a thin stream of oxygenated blood into his mouth to mix with the young man's wad of warm come, and he swallowed everything easily.

When Tyler's cock stopped spasming in his mouth, Moon Doggie drew back, releasing his oral grip on the young man's member. As he did, the tiny wound from which he had drawn Tyler's blood immediately sealed shut.

Moon Doggie's own cock was hard by then, straining for release, and Tyler didn't resist when Moon Doggie flipped the younger man onto his stomach, grabbed his waist, and pulled him up onto his knees. He grabbed a tube of lube from a pocket on the van door and slathered it into Tyler's ass crack before positioning himself behind him. He pressed the head of his cock against the younger man's lube-slickened sphincter, grabbed Tyler's hips, and then pushed forward. The boogie boarder opened to accommodate him and soon Moon Doggie buried his entire length in the younger man's ass.

He held Tyler's hips as he drew back and pushed

forward, fucking the younger man so hard and so fast that the van—even with its specially reinforced suspension system—rocked back and forth. Years had passed since Moon Doggie last took a lover, and despite his other powers, he could not hold back. He came and came hard, firing cool come deep into Tyler's ass, and he held the boogie boarder's cheeks tight against his crotch until his cock ran dry.

Then he pulled back, spun the younger man onto his back and stared into his eyes.

When Tyler awoke in his own bed that afternoon he didn't remember when he'd stepped out of the pale surfer's van, didn't remember the drive home, and didn't remember slipping into his own bed. He did remember the sex and he did remember the way the other man had stared into his eyes.

When he pulled open the curtains, he was surprised by how bright the afternoon sun seemed and he quickly pulled them closed. Though he didn't notice the tiny scab on the underside of his cock where Moon Doggie had sampled his blood as part of a blood-sperm cocktail, he was already experiencing the effects of the nightsurfer's bite.

Tyler remained inside with the curtains closed until it was time for work, and he went through the motions that night without paying much attention to the few tourists who settled onto the stools at the bar and tried to capture his attention. He didn't perk up until he found Moon

Doggie's van parked outside the rear door of Tommy's Tiki Hut when he left work at two a.m.

For the next few hours—and for the next few mornings—they continued their carnal exploration of one another's bodies, and each time Moon Doggie drew just a tiny bit of Tyler's blood, the wound sealing closed as soon as he withdrew the tip of his canine tooth. At home, Tyler stopped opening his curtains, and on the third night he didn't even bother cooking the hamburger meat he'd purchased for dinner.

He blamed the hours spent in Moon Doggie's van for his increasing lethargy but didn't understand why his eyes hurt in even dim sunlight and why he'd developed a taste for steak tartare.

Moon Doggie suggested a visit to the beach for Tyler's first night off from work. He picked the boogie boarder up just after sunset and drove to Hammerhead Beach far south of town.

"I thought no one surfed here," Tyler said as Moon Doggie parked his van behind a line of other vehicles.

"Not everyone is afraid."

Tyler helped Moon Doggie remove the surfboard from the roof of the van, then grabbed their blanket and followed him down to the beach where several nightsurfers and moonbathers had already laid claim to their patches of sand. Unlike every other beach party Tyler had attended, there were no fires and there was no music, only moonlight and the sound of the waves breaking.

The nightsurfers and moonbathers grew restless whenever blood walked among them, and had Tyler accompanied anyone other than Moon Doggie—Hammerhead Beach's Big Kahuna—they might have fallen upon him and torn him asunder. As it was, they just stared as he walked past, making Tyler feel like the Benny he was.

Moon Doggie stopped, had Tyler spread their blanket, and then led him across the beach. After Moon Doggie strapped on his leash, he walked his big gun into the water. When he stood waist deep, he had Tyler climb on the front of the board. Then he climbed on the back and paddled away from the shore, duck diving through a pair of waves until they reached the line-up, and he turned the board toward the shore. That's when Tyler saw the first shark fin slicing through the water in the distance.

"They usually leave us alone, but they know you're here," Moon Doggie said. He snapped up so that he was standing on the board with Tyler still on his knees before him. "Makes me hard just thinking about it."

The bulge in Moon Doggie's baggies emphasized his point and Tyler reached for it. He stroked Moon Doggie's erection through the wet material until Moon Doggie pushed his hand away and freed his cock by shoving his shorts down. As Tyler moved to take the head of Moon Doggie's cock in his mouth, the nightsurfer shifted position to keep the board balanced. At the same time, several moonbathers and nightsurfers lined up along the beach like luminescent Maoi statues staring out at the copulating couple on the surfboard.

Tyler's tongue licked all the way around Moon Doggie's cock, but Moon Doggie wasted no time. He grabbed the back of Tyler's head and shoved his cock all the way into Tyler's oral cavity. He drew back and did it again, face-fucking the younger man hard and fast, oblivious to the ever-increasing number of fins circling the board.

Moon Doggie came hard, erupting within Tyler's mouth, and the younger man could not swallow fast enough to keep the nightsurfer's come from spilling from the corners of his mouth. He drew back quickly, unbalancing the surfboard beneath them. Moon Doggie reflexively adjusted position to keep them from spilling into the water.

"We shouldn't be out here," Tyler said, his gaze following the path of a shark fin that passed only a few feet from the board. "It isn't safe."

"If you were one of us you wouldn't fear our brethren."

"One of you what?"

Moon Doggie explained what he and the creatures lining the beach were. Nightsurfers and moonbathers didn't live in castles, turn into bats, or fear garlic-laden Italian food, but they were every bit as much creatures of the night as popular culture and low-budget horror movies made them out to be. When Moon Doggie finished, Tyler understood his recent lethargy, his aversion to sunlight, and his new dietary desires. He had been changing to become one of them, but he had not completed the transition, a transition to which he had to agree before

Moon Doggie could finish what he had started the first night in the back of his van.

"Join us and experience an endless summer," Moon Doggie offered. "Or take your chances swimming to shore."

Tyler looked at the dozen shark fins circling them and then toward the nightsurfers and moonbathers on the beach, waiting to finish what the sharks might not. "That isn't much of a choice."

Moon Doggie drew one finger along the boogie boarder's jaw line and smiled. "It's the only one you have."

Tyler looked again at his options and then tilted his head back and to the side, exposing his jugular vein.

Moon Doggie had been sloppy the first few times he had tried to convert a hot-blooded lover into a cold-blooded nightsurfer, allowing bloodlust to overcome him. He had accidentally drained his lovers' bodies and had been forced to dispose of them in the ocean as shark chum, just as he had disposed of Wayne's body after his most recent feeding.

This time he was careful. He kissed Tyler's neck, felt the warm blood pulsing beneath the younger man's skin, and then pierced Tyler's jugular vein with both of his needle-sharp canine teeth. He carefully drew out the last of Tyler's lifeblood, replacing it with an eternity as a creature of the night.

As Tyler completed his evolution, the moonbathers and nightsurfers lined up along the shore returned to their blankets, and the sharks circling Moon Doggie's surfboard drifted away.

A few minutes later, the perfect wave lifted Moon Doggie's big gun, and the two nightsurfers rode it into shore.

ABOUT THE AUTHOR

Michael Bracken is the author of several books, but is better known as the author of more than 1,200 short stories, including erotica published in the Lambda Award-nominated anthologies *Show-offs* and *Team Players* and in *Best Gay Erotica 2013, Best New Erotica 4, Fifty Shades of Grey Fedora, Fifty Shades of Green, Flesh & Blood: Guilty as Sin, Gent, Hot Blood: Strange Bedfellows, Oui, Ultimate Gay Erotica 2006,* and many other anthologies and periodicals. Learn more at www.CrimeFictionWriter.com.

PUBLISHING ACKNOWLEDGEMENTS

"Landmark Photography," *Indecent Exposures*, Bruno Gmünder, 2013

"High-Rise Hook-Up," *Hired Hands*, Bruno Gmünder, 2014

"One Hit Wonder," *Rock & Roll Over*, StarBooks Press, 2010

"Total Package," *Best Gay Romance 2010*, Cleis Press, 2010

"Heart On," *Gym Boys*, Cleis Press, 2016

"Honey Do Me," *Under the Desert Sky*, Xcite, 2011

"Young Man's Game," *Model Men*, Cleis Press, 2011

"Dockers," *Nice Butt*, Bold Strokes Books, 2012

"Bathhouse Backstabber," *Men in Love*, Bold Strokes Books, 2016

"Homecoming," *Rookies*, Cleis Press, 2014

"Garden Variety," *All the Boys*, Xcite, 2011

"West Texas Winter," *Cowboy Up*, Cleis Press, 2018

"The Loophole," *Men at Noon, Monsters at Midnight*, StarBooks Press, 2010

"Sporting Wood," *Team Players*, Bruno Gmünder, 2013

"Bareback Rider," *Country Boys*, Cleis Press, 2007

"Slash and Burn," *Boy Fun*, Xcite, 2010

"Tossing the Caber," *Teammates*, StarBooks Press, 2010

"Seven-Inch Stretch," *In Plain View*, Bold Strokes Books, 2011

"Moon Doggie and the Nightsurfers at Hammerhead Beach," *Until the Sun Rises*, Bruno Gmünder, 2014

ALSO FROM MICHAEL BRACKEN

All-American Male
Men in Love and Lust #1

When college student Bernie is dragged to a Christmas party where he knows nobody, the last thing he expects is to be naked and between the thighs of the sexiest man he's ever met.

While older men aren't usually his thing, there's something about Professor Maeyer that gets Bernie going in ways he hasn't felt for a long time. So, when the party ends and everyone's gone home and it's just Bernie and Professor Maeyer, he gets a deeper education, the kind that can't be taught in class, the kind that can only be taught in the bedroom.

Bernie's about to learn just how much Professor Maeyer can blow his mind (and his load).

"Learning Curve" is just one of nineteen scorching hot and smutty-as-hell stories in this sweaty, throbbing, pounding collection of gay erotica from Michael Bracken, acclaimed author of erotic short fiction.

Available now in ebook and paperback

ALSO FROM MICHAEL BRACKEN

Queer Bait
Men in Love and Lust #2

David isn't the hook-up type, but there's something about Clive—the sexy, older man from the pool locker room—that makes David take him up on the offer for drinks.

His hopes of a whirlwind romance, or even just a down-and-dirty afternoon, are dashed when Clive reveals himself to be an undercover cop intent on enlisting David's help. It seems David's new boss has a history of seducing young men, and at least one of them has gone missing, and Clive needs a sexy young man like David to wear a wire and find out just what the man is up to.

Caught between a deadly dangerous boss and a way-too-sexy cop, David has to navigate getting what he wants—Clive inside him—with giving his boss what he wants—him inside David—for information that could save future young gay men.

"Smooth Stroke" is just one of twenty scorching hot and smutty-as-hell stories in this sweaty, throbbing, pounding collection of gay erotica from Michael Bracken, acclaimed author of erotic short fiction.

Available now in ebook and paperback

www.ingramcontent.com/pod-product-compliance
Lightning Source LLC
Chambersburg PA
CBHW030515020726
47494CB00004B/1100